DEAD ON THE DOLMEN

DEAD on the
DOLMEN

An Oscar Tremont Mystery

Cameron
TROST

Dead on the Dolmen
Published by Black Beacon Books
Cover design by Cameron Trost
Copyright © Cameron Trost, 2026

Black Beacon Books
blackbeaconbooks.com

ISBN: 978-0-9756118-4-5

Cameron Trost is an author of mystery, suspense, horror, and post-apocalyptic fiction best known for his puzzles featuring Oscar Tremont, Investigator of the Strange and Inexplicable. He has written four novels, *Dead on the Dolmen*, *Flicker*, *Letterbox*, and *The Tunnel Runner*, and three collections, *Oscar Tremont, Investigator of the Strange and Inexplicable*, *Hoffman's Creeper and Other Disturbing Tales*, and *The Animal Inside*. He runs the independent press, Black Beacon Books, and is a member of the Australian Crime Writers Association and The Short Mystery Fiction Society. Originally from Brisbane, Australia, Cameron lives with his wife and two sons near Guérande in southern Brittany, between the rugged coast and treacherous marshland.

camerontrost.com

1. The Ankou Rides

Doctor David Trevelyan was lying in bed with the duvet pulled up to his neck. His eyes were closed but he hadn't yet managed to fall asleep. The howling of the chill October wind filled his ears. He'd wanted to finish his analysis of the role of the Bugul Noz legend in Breton society but his eyelids had disagreed with him, forcing him to throw in the towel. It didn't matter. The new book was coming along nicely and he'd be able to finish that particular section in the morning. All the ideas were right there in his head and he knew the wording would flow, nudged along by a strong cup of Earl Grey.

As was their habit, the professor of Breton folklore and his son, Rowan, who was studying law, had dined together before going about their separate evening routines. David always watched the BBC World News, which he found more palatable than any of the French equivalents, before retiring upstairs to the small but well-stocked library which lay at the end of the first floor, past the three upstairs bedrooms. Despite the size of Ker Greno—which placed it somewhere between a large house and a manor—the only bathroom was downstairs, and since the two men lived alone together, there was no immediate need for a second one on the first floor. The grand house accommodated all their needs, and the local gardener, Fred Gaillo, came by several times a week to take care of the grounds and undertake any basic maintenance duties.

It was a domestic arrangement that suited both father and son for the time being. Now in his sixties, David Trevelyan had no intention of remarrying, or indeed even getting caught up in what might be labelled *a serious relationship*. The divorce had been difficult on the children initially, but Rowan and Alice—who lived with her husband in Paris—were adults now. Rowan had recently turned thirty and had a girlfriend in Kergaillot, the next village over—just a short walk along the dirt track that led past Ker Greno, before winding through woodlands and following the edge of the marshes. He studied an hour's drive away in Vannes and often spent time with his mother, Anne, and her new boyfriend, Tanguy. They lived on Tanguy's sailing boat in the port of Vannes, using the vessel for day trips and as an oyster bar. Not that either of them was in need of a steady income—it was all about the lifestyle, and Rowan had to admit his mother was far happier now than he remembered her being in the years before the divorce. His father, on the other hand, hadn't changed, despite what Anne said. Rowan had always remembered him being grumpy and stuck in his ways—only really happy when he was researching Breton and Cornish legends or was on the hunt for artefacts.

That night, while the wind howled and whistled through whatever nooks and crannies it found in the structure of Ker Greno, Rowan stayed downstairs by the wood stove to watch the British mystery series, *Vera*. He had a mental list of what he liked and disliked about each parent—the kind of list that writes itself subconsciously and can't be erased—and at the top of that list was the English language. He studied in French, and spoke it with his friends and girlfriend, Youna, but he always preferred to read, listen, speak, and even simply think in English when he could—and when it came to watching a detective drama, there was no question about it. Cradling a dram of his dad's finest whisky, he watched two episodes of *Vera* and managed to place the empty glass on the floor by the sofa before falling asleep during the third. The flickering light from the flames in the wood stove danced on the glass as he slept.

Upstairs, David Trevelyan remained trapped between sleep and wakefulness. He couldn't stop listening to the wind howling outside his window, and he heard those words over and over again, spoken against the wind—almost drowned in it—but always there. The threat. The clear message. His secret had been discovered, and if he didn't want the world to know about it, he'd have to pay up. He could only stall for so long.

A violent gust shook the window. Most of the other families in the village closed the shutters at night, but that was a habit David had never adopted. He didn't like the thought of being locked up like that and not knowing what was happening outside. The prospect bugged him—the idea that when the sun rose in the morning, he'd still be in the dark. It wasn't natural. In any case, the shutters rattled just as much in the wind as the window panes. When the wind from the Mor Bras picked up, there was no escaping its mighty music.

He was being blackmailed for a lot of money. Even if it had been half as much—not reaching those impressive six digits—he would still have hesitated. It wasn't so much the amount that mattered as the principle. It was a betrayal. A brazen and unapologetic kick in the teeth. Should he pay it? There wasn't really any other option, except—well, except that obvious and drastic one.

He rolled onto his side and pulled his duvet up over his left shoulder, but his head didn't have enough support, so he fluffed his pillow. He made himself as comfortable as possible and tried to convince himself he'd be able to fall asleep if he was lying in the right position. But sleep didn't come. The howling wind and threatening words bound him.

The clock was ticking. This was no bluff. An answer had to be given.

You have one week. Only two days remained.

David rolled onto his back, shoved the duvet down to his waist, and drew a deep breath. He felt smothered. He almost wanted to open the window and let the wind fill the room. Instead, he lay there and stared into the darkness where he knew the ceiling to be. The bedroom was in darkness except for a rectangle of light showing him where the window was. Outside, the faintest glimmer of light brushed the night sky, hinting at the presence of a hesitant moon up there somewhere.

While writing, he could ignore those dreadful words, but in bed, they filled his mind, fanned by the wind.

Then there were those other sounds. He didn't know when they'd first reached his ears, but they were growing steadily louder, and they sent a chill to the bone. At first, he thought he must have fallen asleep and started dreaming, but when his body responded to the command to sit up, push the duvet aside, and swing his legs over the side of the bed, he knew he was awake.

'Turn that off and go to bed, Rowan!'

Thirty years old or not, Rowan was still his son and living rent-free in the Trevelyan family home. On top of that, David hadn't failed to notice the level of liquid gold in his whisky collection gradually descending. At least the lad's mother had taught him to cook before running away with Popeye the Sailor Man.

'Rowan! Did you hear me?'

There was no answer from downstairs. The distinctive grinding of cartwheels and the tattoo of hooves on gravel continued.

David switched his beside lamp on and got out of bed. He was about to head to the bedroom door when understanding dawned. He couldn't tell whether he'd seen a movement out of the corner of his eye first or merely realised the sound wasn't coming from downstairs—but from outside. All he knew was that he found his attention drawn to the window.

'What the devil's going on?' he whispered to himself.

His bare feet carried him half a dozen shuffled steps across the polished wood floor to the window, through which he could see the treetops being whipped about in the wind, losing their yellowed leaves. The tips of bare branches danced maniacally. Then David's gaze turned down to the dirt path and his hazel eyes beheld a sight that stabbed him through with pure terror and gripped his mind— his clever, analytical mind—with a steely, numbing grasp.

He opened his mouth to speak, but his jaw bobbed uselessly like flotsam in a stormy sea.

It had come to a halt in front of the dolmen, which stood between the dirt track and the woods. That single horizontal slab of granite lying across two standing stones was by far the oldest manmade structure in the village of Greno—and somehow, this dark figure looked just as ageless.

12

David recognised it immediately, and yet it was impossible.

Was this a bizarre joke? Someone in training for Halloween? But the local youngsters weren't capable of playing a trick like this. Every detail was chillingly accurate—just as legend had it.

The figure wore a long black coat and a black hat with a brim so broad it blocked David's view of the head. The two tassels which were the ends of the hatband were whipped about by the wind, and the silver buckle in the middle of the hatband shone under the haunting yellow light provided by the small cart's two lamps, which hung from upright posts. One black horse was attached to the cart, and it waited patiently.

'The Ankou!' David mouthed, hardly daring to utter the horrid name, and as if hearing him, the head rose, looking straight up at the bedroom window. Its face was a gleaming skull with empty eye sockets as black as abandoned wells.

David gasped as it raised the cruel, curved scythe into the air and slashed wildly in his direction.

He stumbled back into his room, all but collapsing onto his bed, and before he could return to the window, the horrific grinding of cartwheels and tapping of hooves had started again.

He craned his neck to watch the cart go trundling along the track and disappear out of view. The last glimpse he caught was of the wicked scythe glowing in the glimmering light of the two swinging kerosene lamps.

The threatening words played in his mind again, more distant and vague now. But it didn't make sense. Why dress up as the Ankou—the collector of souls? This wasn't the blackmailer's style.

He stared down to the where the faint outline of the dolmen could only just be made out. The solid stone structure hardly seemed to be there at all.

How long he stood there at the window, knees shaking and mind stunned, he couldn't say. He was losing his grip on reality, but at least he was aware of that. He wasn't yet beyond the point of no return. After a few long seconds, he managed to sit himself on the edge of his bed, gather his wits, and force reason to take the reins

13

once again.

The sounds that had accompanied the Ankou's appearance were now gone, and David found himself wondering whether it had really happened at all. But he wasn't asleep, so it hadn't been a nightmare. He was sitting there on the edge of his bed, wide awake and listening to the wind. It had happened—*something* had happened—but what exactly?

He remembered his grandfather, all those years ago in Cornwall, telling him tales by the fireplace. As a boy, he'd likened Grandpa Trevelyan to a steam train—the clay pipe in his mouth puffing whenever he paused for dramatic effect, the white mutton chops like steam on either side of his chin, and those coal-dark eyes—eyes that glowed when the old man turned to stare into the fire, as though drawing inspiration from it. The old man had told the legends with such earnestness and zeal that the young David had believed every word, and even now, he wondered whether his grandfather had truly believed the legends himself.

He got to his feet and edged closer to the window again until he could see the dolmen. It stood alone and undisturbed—steadfast and timeless.

Ankou in Breton. *Ankow* in Cornish. David had recognised him immediately. The Grim Reaper was the popular term used in Victorian ghost stories and tacky costume shops, but the origin of the Ankou could be traced back to Arawn, the king of the otherworld.

As he stood staring at the dolmen, David began to wonder whether his obsession had finally taken its toll on his mental health. He'd always approached the study of folklore from a scientific angle, analysing the cultural role of legends. He was a man of research and reason, not nocturnal hallucinations.

'Did you really see it?' he whispered.

The only answer was the howling wind, taunting him.

He told himself he ought to grab a torch and something heavy—like the cast-iron frying pan he'd bought from Thérèse Derrien at the last village flea market—and go after the fiend. But he'd never been a brave man, and even less so a stupid one. If he hadn't imagined it, and this wasn't someone's bizarre idea of a pre-Halloween joke, what then? Even if he somehow caught up with the cart, he wouldn't stand a chance.

He told himself he should have taken a photo. That was the only way to be certain. He'd left his phone in the library. In fact, he kept a proper camera with telescopic lens on top of the bookshelf beside his writing desk. It was too late now though. Too late for tonight.

What if—? He shook his head. But the question remained. What if it was to happen again?

David stood and walked to the window without really knowing why. He simply couldn't bear to stay perched on the edge of his bed, and he definitely wasn't ready to crawl under the duvet again. He watched the treetops thrashing about in the wind and he stared at the dolmen. He was yearning to do something—to act, but he couldn't even think straight. All he knew was that he wasn't insane. With every breath, he grew more certain of that. It had happened. The question that remained was—why?

When he was ready, he stepped back from the window, turned around, and slowly made his way to the bedroom door. He needed to go to the toilet and drink a glass of water.

He felt his way along the corridor, and when he reached the suit of armour standing guard in a shallow recess at the end, he turned left and made his way down the stairs. There was enough light from the TV and the dying embers in the wood stove to let him see that Rowan was sleeping on the sofa. He shook his head as he picked the whisky glass off the floor and placed it quietly on the kitchen table before pouring himself a glass of water. Once he'd drunk enough water, he went to the toilet, looked at his expressionless face in the bathroom mirror for a minute, and made his way back, switching the TV off before climbing the stairs. He doubted he'd get much sleep, but he was ready to try.

15

2. Cold Light of Morning

Rowan was making a pot of coffee when David came downstairs.

'Hi, Dad.'

'Good morning. You're up early for a Saturday.'

'I fell asleep pretty early.'

'So I noticed.'

'You don't look like you slept too well.'

David didn't reply. He took a teabag from the box on the kitchen counter, fixed himself a cup of Earl Grey, and stared through the window. Dewdrops glistened on broad hydrangea leaves and a robin chirped from the wicker-like branches of the salt cedar growing in the middle of the garden.

Rowan watched his father stare through the window. 'Everything good, Dad?'

David turned to his son, jiggled his teabag thoughtfully, and looked at the living area. He was going to mention his whisky collection but decided against it.

'Fine,' he said eventually. 'I need to get on with my writing this morning.'

'I won't bother you. I'm off to see Youna. I might stay the night at her place.'

David sipped his tea and looked Rowan in the eyes as he did so.

'That doesn't bother you?'

'Why would it bother me? You're young and in love. Enjoy it while it lasts.'

Rowan shook his head, then poured himself a mug of coffee from the French press. 'I just wanted to make sure you didn't need company.'

David placed his cup on the bench, yawned, and rubbed his face.

'What are you saying, Rowan? It's too early for riddles.'

'Nothing, Dad. Forget it. I thought you might be worried about something.'

David pinched the bridge of his nose between thumb and forefinger. 'I didn't sleep so well—that's all.'

'Not surprising with some nutter riding around in a chariot in the middle of the night.'

Rowan noted his father's look of surprise and the fact that he almost knocked his cup over as he took it from the bench and drank.

'Did you hear what I said?'

'I don't think I heard you right, Rowan.' David faked a laugh. 'It sounded to me like you said you heard a chariot race during the night. You might want to go easy on my whisky.'

'Oh, yeah—that's it.' He rolled his eyes. 'I drank a couple of drams and imagined hearing horses and wagon wheels. Happens to me all the time.'

'Look—I don't know what you think you heard.'

Rowan looked his father in the eye. It was clear he was lying.

'You heard it,' was all he said.

David sipped his tea. The muffled chirping of the robin outside was the only sound that broke the silence.

'Dad,' Rowan said. 'I know you. No one knows you better.'

'You believe that?'

'I'm pretty sure I know you better than Mum ever did.'

David scoffed. 'And yet you're still here.'

'I'm only here for your whisky.'

David grinned. 'You've certainly inherited my caustic sense of humour.'

'Or your blunt honesty.'

David laughed. 'I'm bluntly honest now, am I?'

'On second thoughts, no—that you are not. I think there's a lot you don't tell me.'

'Look, Rowan, I'm barely awake. It's a bit early for all these mind games.'

'Mind games? All I said was that I'm not surprised you're tired what with the nocturnal disturbance.'

'What exactly did you hear?' David asked, and as he sipped his tea, he leaned back against the kitchen bench, bracing himself for his son's answer.

'Hooves beating and the grinding of wheels against gravel. It came from the path to the marshland. I'd guess one horse.'

'That's insane,' David said. 'You must have imagined it. You were probably dreaming.'

Rowan held his father's gaze without saying a word.

'What do you want me to say?' David asked.

'I know you heard it too and I know you got out of bed to look out the bedroom window.'

'You don't know that.'

'Yes,' Rowan insisted. 'I know you better than anyone else. So?'

'So—what?'

'What did you see, Dad?'

David sighed. 'Can you at least make yourself useful and scramble some eggs first?'

Rowan nodded slowly, not taking his eyes off his father. 'Deal,' he said.

There was just enough milk and eggs left in the fridge, and plenty of salted butter.

I've cracked the stubborn old man, Rowan thought to himself as he cracked the eggs and emptied them into a bowl. David was staring out the window again, contemplating the dewdrops and getting his story straight in his head. It was a still morning—the calm after the storm.

Once the scrambled eggs were ready, Rowan sprinkled some parmesan over the top and placed the frying pan on a wooden chopping board. David took two plates and forks from the antique cherry cupboard and held them out for his son to serve the scrambled eggs.

After the first mouthful, David nodded appreciatively at Rowan.

'Good?'

'That hits the spot.'

Rowan took a mouthful and looked at his father expectantly.

David took another sip of tea before broaching the topic of the nocturnal incident. 'I didn't see much.'

'What *did* you see? There was a horse and a cart of some kind, wasn't there?'

David nodded. 'Yes.'

'I didn't imagine it after all. I knew I hadn't.'

'No,' David mused. 'We couldn't have both imagined it.'

'Who was it?'

David put a forkful of scrambled eggs into his mouth to buy some time. 'I didn't get a chance to see,' he said eventually.

Rowan narrowed his eyes. 'But there was a pause. The hoof beats and grinding of the wheels stopped for a while. It wasn't until they started again that I knew I hadn't imagined it.'

'You didn't look outside?'

Rowan shook his head.

'He stopped by the dolmen,' David admitted.

'He?'

'Or *she*, Rowan. I don't know. I just said *he* because I had to choose a pronoun, didn't I? Is the interrogation over?'

Rowan shrugged. 'Strange—that's all.'

'That it is.'

'Why ride around in a horse-drawn cart at night and stop by the dolmen?'

'Why indeed?'

'The dolmen is in line with your bedroom window,' Rowan observed.

'Correct.'

He raised his eyebrows at his father. 'This person didn't look up? You didn't see his face?'

'It was the middle of the night during a storm, Rowan.'

'I know. But there was bright moonlight.'

'I'm aware the moon is in a waning gibbous phase, but that doesn't change the fact that I didn't see his face. I don't know who

19

it was. Can we let it rest at that?'

'Okay. Fine.' Rowan shoved a forkful of scrambled eggs into his mouth.

'I'm going to get back to my writing.'

'I'll leave you to it,' Rowan said.

'Don't forget your key in case you come back from Youna's during the night.'

'I won't. No more nocturnal disturbances for you, Dad.'

'I'd appreciate that.' David ate his last mouthful of scrambled eggs and finished his tea. He put the plate and fork in the dishwasher and left the empty cup on the kitchen bench. Before heading back upstairs, he turned to Rowan and said, 'Lock the door behind you when you leave.'

'I will,' Rowan answered with a frown, but David was already climbing the staircase.

#

It was with its usual sluggish calm that the village of Greno came to life on that damp October morning. Like Rowan and David, most of the inhabitants were taking their breakfast, albeit in their more modest thatched cottages. Arnaud and Nina Moison—whose house was separated from Ker Greno by the marshland path—were sipping black coffee and checking their social media profiles while their children watched the morning cartoons and enjoyed toasted croissants and orange juice. Outside the next cottage over, separated from the Moisons by a laurel hedge, Kevin Barazer was leaning against the whitewashed stone wall and smoking the first cigarette of the day. His Irish setters, Ruby and Cayenne, were standing in the doorway, eager to go for a walk.

The only people already up and about were Thérèse Derrien, the widow who lived in the cottage boasting the village's finest flower garden and vegetable patch, and Fred Gaillo, the local gardener and handyman. Thérèse had gone to check on her hens and gather eggs and Fred was on his way to Ker Greno to do his fortnightly upkeep.

There was always plenty of trimming and raking to do after a storm.

Fred Gaillo had long scruffy hair that fell around his shoulders in a brown tangle and eyes the colour of oak leaves in autumn. He wore the same dark green jumper and old jeans he always wore when gardening, and he wore his usual expression—a kind of wistful, faraway look. The battered old wheelbarrow he was pushing contained the tools needed for the morning's work. The petrol hedge trimmer, stepladder, and rake rattled as he made his way along the street and stopped at the hedge delineating the grounds of Ker Greno. He glanced along the drive and past the salt cedar before starting up the hedge trimmer.

Rowan appeared just as he'd just finished trimming the entrance to the drive and cleaning up around the letterbox so the postman wouldn't have to negotiate overhanging laurel branches and thorny brambles when delivering mail.

'Hi, Fred.'

'How's it going, Rowan?'

'Can't complain.'

'The old man writing?'

'You know it,' Rowan said, looking back at the house.

'It was blowing a right gale last night. Any damage around the house?'

'Not that I've noticed. There are some small branches on the lawn and plenty of leaves, but nothing else.'

'I'll check it out.'

Rowan was about to say goodbye and head to the marshland path when Fred noticed his hesitation.

'You look like you've got something on your mind?'

'Yeah,' Rowan said, stretching the word out. 'I guess I have.'

'Anything I can help with?'

He shook his head and started to walk away.

'Your dad giving you grief?'

He stopped. 'He's always been a bit of a grumpy old so-and-so.'

'No comment.'

Rowan nodded. 'Only—I get the feeling he's not telling me

something.'

'Why do you say that?'

'I don't know.'

'Not telling you about what exactly?'

'Well, that's the thing. I really don't know. He's being a bit vague. His mind is on his work. There's nothing new there, but it's been getting worse over the last few days.'

Fred looked to the ground and frowned. 'You think he might have a dark secret or two. That's what you're suggesting?'

'I'm obviously not the only one asking himself that question then.'

The gardener looked up at Rowan and raised his eyebrows. 'What I can tell you is that you are your own man. We're not responsible for our fathers' mistakes and we're only doomed to repeat them if we allow it. That much I do know.'

Rowan drew a deep breath and made a mental note not to forget those words. He then went ahead and asked Fred about the strange occurrence.

'Did you hear any unusual noises last night?'

'You're not talking about the wind?'

'No. That's not what I mean.'

'I'm a pretty sound sleeper, Rowan. What kind of unusual noise are you talking about?'

Rowan groaned. He wasn't sure if he wanted to say, but he'd brought the topic up and couldn't back out now.

'It wasn't Arnaud and Nina having a row, was it?'

'A horse and cart,' Rowan said, studying Fred's face for a reaction.

'A horse and cart? What time was this?'

'I don't know. In the middle of the night.'

'Unusual indeed.'

'Yeah,' Rowan said. 'Both Dad and I heard it.'

'I don't think anyone in the village has a cart or wagon of any description. Did you see it?'

'Dad saw it but couldn't see who it was.'

Fred ran a gloved hand over his frizzy mane and made a clicking

22

sound with his tongue.

'I don't know what to make of it,' Rowan said.

'I'm racking my brains but can't imagine who has a horse-drawn cart and would ride around in it in the middle of a storm. It's hardly the behaviour of a sane person, is it?'

Rowan shook his head.

'I'll let you know if I hear anything.'

'Please do. I'd better let you get back to work.'

'And you—off to see your girl in Kergaillot?'

'You know it.' Rowan winked before heading off to the path.

'Good for you,' Fred said and started his hedge trimmer up again.

When Rowan reached the dolmen, he stopped and looked up at his father's bedroom window. A fleeting movement nearby caught his eye, but there was nothing left to be seen by the time he'd turned to look at the library window. Nevertheless, he couldn't shake off the impression it was his father he'd glimpsed standing there, staring down at the dolmen.

He turned to look at the ancient stone structure but it was even more unyielding than his father. There were hoof marks along the gravel path—undeniably fresh ones—and lines that could certainly have been caused by hard, narrow wheels.

He looked at the library window again but caught sight of no movement this time, so he continued on his way.

Snapped branches and dead leaves littered the path ever more densely as he walked. Birds frolicked in the trees and a field mouse darted across the path. It was a normal autumn morning.

Once the path curved left and led into the woodlands, where the branches of trees on either side reached overhead with skeletal fingers seeking contact, Rowan remembered there was one person who was more likely to have heard the horse and cart than anyone else—the hermit who lived in a tattered caravan in the woods, wedged between the path and the marsh.

'Hey, Brieg,' he called to the hunched figure in the ditch on the left-hand side of the path.

The hermit turned around and stared narrow-eyed at Rowan for a

23

moment before raising the basket in his hand.

'Want some mushrooms, rich boy?'

'Not today. Thanks.'

Brieg shrugged. He was wearing a filthy beige coat that had probably belonged to a city professional many years ago and a bright floral foulard. What looked like a black skirt but was more likely a nightgown or cloak hung around his knees, and on his feet he wore black boots with long red socks. A black beanie covered his head and a grizzled goatee adorned his chin. Rowan didn't know how old he was and had never dared ask. Middle-aged? He could have been younger. His weather-beaten face and calloused hands made it hard to tell.

'No problem with the storm?'

'I never have problems with storms. So long as a tree doesn't get blown over and crush me in my sleep. You sure you don't want any mushrooms? I don't pick any particularly poisonous ones.' He shot Rowan a cheeky grin.

'I'm good. You didn't happen to hear the horse and cart last night?'

Brieg bent over and picked a mushroom, which he dropped into his basket.

'Did you hear me?'

'What's that about a horse?'

'A horse and cart came along this path in the middle of the night.'

Brieg shook his head. 'And they call *me* the crazy one. What have you been smoking, lad?'

'I haven't been smoking. I heard a horse and cart during the night.'

'Did you see it?'

'My dad did.'

'Did he now? Tell him to be careful it's not the Ankou out for his soul.'

'Very funny.'

But Brieg wasn't laughing. 'There was no horse and cart here last night, young Rowan, and don't you go telling yourself otherwise.

Best get those ideas out of your head, and if you can't, keep them to yourself.'

'Understood,' Rowan replied, knowing there was no use pushing the matter and upsetting the hermit.

'If you hear it again,' Brieg went on, examining the gills of the slender grey mushroom he'd just picked from near the base of an elm tree, 'my advice is to stay inside and make sure the doors and windows are securely locked.'

'What?'

'You heard me, Milord.'

'You're worse than my father if you actually believe these legends.'

'If he doesn't believe them, why has he spent so many years studying them, writing about them, and giving lectures on them?'

Rowan sighed. 'He's interested in the influence they had on Cornish and Breton culture. They're of immense sociological value.'

Brieg rolled his eyes. 'Right. As simple as that, is it?'

'Yeah, it is,' Rowan insisted. 'Whoever's behind this is a human being, made of flesh and blood. It's most likely some joker training for Halloween.'

Brieg stared at him wide-eyed. 'You can't be serious. You think it's someone training for Halloween? I know that ridiculous American celebration is growing in popularity every year, but what was the scariest costume you saw last year—a ten-year-old wearing a werewolf mask?'

Rowan felt like telling him that *he* was the most unsettling presence in Greno at any time of the year, but thought better of it. Instead, he told him he was right.

'I don't know what to believe, but if there's someone riding around in a horse-drawn cart in the middle of the night, I'd play it safe, and the safest of the safe is to turn a blind eye.'

'Is that what you're doing by telling me you didn't hear a thing last night?'

'I'm telling you to lay off the herb.' He gave Rowan an enigmatic smile and passed the mushroom under his nose. 'This is nature's good stuff.'

Rowan heard branches crack underfoot behind him. He turned to see Kevin Barazer approaching. Ruby and Cayenne were trotting along behind him, stopping here and there to sniff at the ground.

'Turn a blind eye,' Brieg repeated quietly.

Rowan's brow creased.

'What are you two up to? An unlikely duo if ever there was one— the village freak and the English playboy.'

'Give it a rest, Kevin!' Brieg jeered. 'He's only half English.'

They all laughed.

'Half Cornish and half Breton to be precise,' Rowan told them.

'That's the spirit,' Kevin said. 'What's new with you two anyway?'

Rowan and Brieg looked each other in the eye. 'Nothing,' Rowan said. 'Just having a look at Brieg's mushrooms.'

'Trade you three for three smokes?' Kevin asked.

'Got yourself a deal,' Brieg replied, trudging up onto the path to show him the harvest.

'Quite a storm last night,' Kevin said, inspecting the mushrooms. 'I could have sworn I heard some idiot racing about on a horse,' he added casually.

'Is that so?' Rowan asked, giving Brieg a sideways glance.

'Might have imagined it, of course, but I could have sworn I did.'

'The wind can make strange sounds sometimes,' Brieg suggested.

Kevin shrugged. 'These three look good.' He took a pack of rollies from his jacket pocket and handed three to the hermit.

'A pleasure doing business with you.'

'Likewise,' Kevin said. 'You're both welcome to drop by for a drink of an evening, you know.'

'Lonely since your split-up?' Brieg asked.

'Sometimes, but I'm better off that way. These two females are the loves of my life. Take them for a walk and tell them they're good girls at least once a day and they're happy. You two never get lonely, I take it?'

'The trees are all the company I need,' Brieg said. There was a glint in his eyes as he surveyed the woodland around him. 'And this

26

lad's off to visit his sweetheart.'

'Is that why you're always walking this way? You got yourself a little lady in Kergaillot?'

Rowan nodded and couldn't help but grin.

'That's a relief. I was beginning to think you had designs on this weirdo.'

'Lay off it,' Brieg said. 'I'm asexual and this boy's as straight as an arrow.'

'I'm just messing with you,' Kevin said, slapping Rowan on the back. 'Anyway, the girls are getting restless. Catch you both later.'

'I'm off as well,' Rowan told Brieg as Kevin hurried after Ruby and Cayenne. 'I'll keep what you said in mind.'

'You do that—and keep an eye on that father of yours.'

'Do you know something?' Rowan asked. 'You'd tell me if you did?'

'I would, but I don't *know* anything. I *sense* things. When you live between the woods and the marshes, you learn to trust your senses and follow your nose.'

Rowan nodded. They sounded like wise words. He had to trust his senses, and above all, he sensed that his father wasn't being open with him. And that, for the moment, was all he could sense.

3. The Oak

David got out of his chair, stretched his arms over his head, and walked over to the window again. He had to admit it was a relief when his son was out of the house. The clock was ticking and his blackmailer wasn't going to hold off much longer. When it came to the crunch and a decision had to be made, he didn't want Rowan around. Whatever happened, he didn't want his son to know the truth.

The dolmen stood alone, filtered sunlight adding at least an impression of warmth to the cold stone. The bare treetops that had been dancing frenetically to the storm's wild music were now dormant. The stillness was disturbed only by robins and finches flitting from branch to branch and dropping to the ground in search of worms and insects left exposed by the storm.

David had made progress with his writing, and already had the closing sentences of the section he was working on completed in his mind.

Anatole Le Braz reminds us in his introductory letter to the Breton chapter of "The Fairy-Faith in Celtic Countries" [11] *that the Bugul Noz's hideous appearance is in fact a salutary attribute for mankind. Whereas ugliness is so often connected to maliciousness in folk legend, here we have a benevolent fairy that by repelling us protects us from the dangers of the forest at night. Mere days before writing this chapter, there was a news report that a wolf was found dead on a road near Rennes, confirming the rumours that this wild woodland animal has made its reappearance in Brittany—if indeed it had ever completely vanished. Despite the unfortunate end met by this particular creature, we are reassured by this good news on the biodiversity front. It is also, however, a clear reminder of just how dangerous the woods at night must have been regarded in days gone by and that the Bugul Noz, by using its frightful appearance to scare us away, earns its name which in English becomes Night Shepherd. Breton folklore teaches us an important lesson here which is as true today as it ever was. Don't be too hasty to judge by appearances.*

David closed his eyes and the image of the Ankou appeared. The skeletal face turned to look up at him frozen at his bedroom window, and the scythe slashed in his direction.

'Not all lessons can be applied to all situations,' he found himself whispering as he opened his eyes to peer down at the dolmen. The legend of the Ankou was not that of the Bugul Noz. Its appearance only ever foretold one outcome—death.

He walked around the library. Standing at the window had become unbearable, and he wasn't ready to settle down behind his laptop again. He needed to stretch his legs. He simply needed to keep moving. But his feet took him past the bookshelves and across the room to another window, the one that overlooked the garden and drive. He drew a deep breath as he watched Fred, who was standing on an unseen ladder, slowly swinging his hedge trimmer along the top of the hedge. He was quite the gardener. There was no doubt about that. One might even go so far as to call him an artist of sorts.

David released his breath and laughed one single, hollow laugh. Was this the Ankou, petrifying him in the middle of the night and now trimming his laurel hedge? It didn't make an ounce of sense, did it? But then, people didn't always make sense. Fred had already shown how unpredictable he could be, but here he was doing the gardening as though everything was just fine, knowing he'd not just get the job done but done remarkably well and that David would pay him the agreed price—cash in hand. Business as usual.

He decided to go downstairs to make himself another cup of tea. From the kitchen window, all he could see was the blade of the hedge trimmer moving along as though of its own volition.

An idea occurred to David as he filled the kettle. Were people capable of being unpredictable? Did anyone ever truly act out of character? He couldn't help but wonder. He had his character, and everyone always expected him to behave according to it. Of that he was quite certain. While he waited for the water to boil, he stared at the longcase clock by the wood stove. Through the muffled drone of the hedge trimmer, the growing sound of boiling water, and the faint birdsong from the salt cedar, he could hear it ticking.

#

There was a knock at the bedroom door, accompanied by giggling. 'Are you two staying in bed all day?' Louane asked.

There was no answer.

'I guess they are,' Gwen said, and the cousins giggled.

'Give us a minute!' Youna complained from the bedroom, her voice muffled.

'Did you say to give you a minute?' Louane asked. 'Mum always taught us not to talk with our mouths full, remember? It's rude.'

'Sod off, Louane!'

'Pretty sure Aunty Pauline would spank you if she heard you use that kind of language,' Gwen couldn't help adding.

'Spanking?' Louane spat. 'Hah—don't go giving Rowan any more ideas. He has plenty of his own by the sound of it!'

They burst out laughing and didn't stop when the bedroom door came swinging open. Youna was wrapped in a white bed sheet but her face—framed by a mess of bottle-blonde hair—was a good deal redder than usual.

'Whoa! Calm down, little sister,' Louane said, taking a step back. 'We're just having a laugh. You finished, lover boy?'

'For the time being.'

Louane and Gwen laughed hysterically and Youna spun around to glare at him. When she turned back to her sister and cousin, she forced a smile and asked them if there was hot coffee in the pot.

Gwen saluted her. 'I'll brew some more, on the double.'

'That's more like it,' Youna said, stepping out and closing the door behind her so Rowan could get dressed in privacy. 'I'm having a quick shower.'

'You do that,' Louane said.

30

Rowan emerged from the bedroom a moment later.

'Planning on staying inside all day?' Gwen asked.

'I've already been out for a nice walk this morning, unlike you ladies.'

'Well, you're going to have to do it again.'

'We could go for a bike ride instead,' Louane suggested.

'Let's do that,' Gwen agreed. 'More coffee first though.'

Time always seemed to stand still for Rowan when he was with Youna, Louane, and Gwen. They all got along so well, and even when they got on each others' nerves, it blew over quickly. There was never any lingering animosity. Louane was engaged and Gwen had a boyfriend of her own, both living in Nantes, so Rowan and Youna often had the house to themselves. That, of course, was nice, but it got a bit too quiet for Youna when the others were away for several days at a time and Rowan was at university in Vannes. He could appreciate that—a little too much like living at Ker Greno.

As Gwen poured him a cup of coffee, he thought about bringing up what had happened during the storm, but Brieg's words were ringing in his ears. If he was right and turning a blind eye was the safest option, it would be wise not to mention the matter at all. And so he kept quiet about it, letting Louane and Gwen discuss where they could all go for a ride while he sipped his coffee in silence. But while he didn't voice his thoughts, he couldn't stop himself from thinking about his father. The coachman had stopped outside his window and Rowan didn't know what had happened at that moment. He'd given his father no choice but to admit he'd witnessed the halt, but he hadn't succeeded in eliciting any further details from him.

'Are you interested, Rowan?' Gwen asked.

'Sorry. What was that?'

'A ride through Trébrezan and back through La Lande to *Le Chêne* for a well-earned drink.'

'That sounds perfect,' he replied.

Gwen and Louane continued talking and he let his thoughts drift back to his father as he sipped his coffee. He'd said he couldn't

31

recognise the coachman, but Rowan wasn't sure he believed him.

'What's wrong?' Louane asked, but he didn't hear her at first.

When he realised they were both looking at him, he opened his mouth to speak, but at that moment, Youna came out of the bathroom, washed and dressed.

'I'm fine,' he said.

'You look a little worried,' Gwen said.

'Why would I be?'

'Is it your dad?' Louane asked.

He frowned. 'Why do you say that?'

Louane shrugged. 'Who else could it be?'

'He—you know what he's like, Youna—he can be a pain in the arse sometimes.'

'Hey, that's no way to talk about my little sister's future father-in-law!'

That made Rowan laugh.

'We'll see, Louane,' Youna said, and Rowan caught the mischievous glint in her eye. 'I suspect Professor Trevelyan no longer believes in the institution of marriage.'

'I have no doubt about it,' Rowan said.

'He doesn't approve of me?'

'You know perfectly well that's not it, Youna. He approves no less of you than of anyone else. In fact, he quite likes you. You're right though—he doesn't have much faith in marriage.'

'He's getting you down?' Gwen asked.

'The same as usual. I'm fine, really.'

Rowan knew that if the three of them kept pressing the matter, he'd end up mentioning the incident, and for a reason he couldn't quite wrap his head around, he'd taken it upon himself to take Brieg's advice. His strange talk of the Ankou and his insistence on pushing the whole business from his mind had bothered him more than he cared to admit. The more he thought about, the more adamant he became that the hermit couldn't possibly have failed to be woken by the horse and cart trundling past his ramshackle caravan.

'Let's get moving,' Gwen chirped, eager to wash the gloomy mood away.

'Where are we going?' Youna raised her palms. 'Whatever happened to consultation?'

'Consultation?' Louane scoffed. 'Get off it, sis. What are we—the United Nations? You choose to have a post-coital shower, you miss out on the vote.'

Youna laughed. 'Whatever you say. What's the plan?'

'A lovely little bike ride followed by refreshments at *Le Chêne.*'

'You up for it, Rowan?'

'Oh, he's up for another ride,' Gwen answered before bursting out laughing.

'You two need to grow up,' Youna said, shaking her head. 'Honestly, and to think I'm the youngest.'

'Don't be such a spoilsport,' Louane said, getting up and grabbing her coat. 'Let's go!'

Rowan finished his now cold coffee and was the first outside. He opened the garage and took the spare bicycle. It was older and in poorer shape than the other three but the wheels turned and the brakes worked well enough. Louane locked the front door behind her and Rowan closed the garage door once the others had taken their bicycles.

The sky was clearing and only a light breeze swept across the landscape. They pedalled down the street out of Kergaillot and turned right to pass through Kerhaut and onto the unsealed marshland track. Unlike Greno, the other villages in the area were made up not only of uninhabited ruins and thatched cottages but also modern houses with smooth, angular walls and large windows that made those unaccustomed to them think of aquariums. These villages were little more than a dozen houses lining a single street barely wide enough in places for two cars to cross paths.

As they rode past a newly-built house with an ancient stone oven standing sentry by its short pebble drive, Rowan took his jacket off and flung it over his left shoulder. The only reminder of last night's storm was the carpet of leaves, twigs, and branches that grew thicker as they continued up the gentle slope out of Kerhaut. It was here that the unsealed track began and hedgerows and trees replaced houses.

As he rode, Rowan couldn't help but glance every now and then at the ground whenever they reached a particularly damp stretch of track, wondering if he'd catch sight of hoof marks and the kind of thin rut only a cartwheel could leave.

'Who's up for a sprint to the Trébrezan junction?' Gwen shouted as they reached the point where the track curved left onto a long, straight stretch. Although she was more solidly built than her cousins, she was undoubtedly the most athletic of the three, and it was only once in a blue moon that Rowan could beat her. Nevertheless, it was bad form to turn down a challenge, so everyone immediately started pedalling as hard as they could.

Gwen skid to a halt and grinned like the child who'd got the biggest piece of cake as Rowan, Louane, and lastly Youna reached her.

'Youna's shout at *Le Chêne*,' Gwen teased.

'With pleasure, but on one condition—we don't do any more sprints,' Youna replied.

'Agreed,' Gwen said. 'Anyway, you've had your fair share of exercise this morning.'

Rowan rolled his eyes. 'Let's keep moving.'

They headed along the track to the left, moving away from the marshland where reeds were swaying in the breeze and a grey heron was fishing. The track to Trébrezan was particularly damp at the start. There was a pond on one side and a row of enormous maritime pines on the other. Sunlight almost never touched the ground here, so the track was damp until it opened out and later became a sealed street where the houses began. Rowan studied the ground as he rode, negotiating the dips and troughs of the track. It was clear to see that no vehicle of any kind had passed this way recently.

He lagged a little behind as he tried to imagine where the cart could have gone after the halt at the dolmen. There was no doubt in his mind that it had passed Brieg's caravan, because there was simply nowhere it could have left the path between Ker Greno and where the hermit lived. Rowan couldn't for the life of him see where it could have left the path before Kergaillot either. He decided that once they were at the bar, drinks in hand, he'd broach the topic of the storm and see if one of them would remember having heard unusual activity during the night. The three of them were sound sleepers. That he knew. But there was always a chance. He wouldn't have to admit anything himself. The mere fact of knowing that someone in Kergaillot had heard the cart was all he needed.

He caught up with the group shortly after the stone cross in Trébrezan and they pumped their legs as they climbed the gentle slope leading through the village until the street flattened out. A couple of minutes later, they reached the junction with La Lande, and a minute after that they arrived at *Le Chêne*, the bar which marked the entrance to Greno, standing at the other end of the street from Ker Greno. Rowan had almost completed a loop that morning since leaving the house. The stretch between the bar and Ker Greno—effectively the entire length of the village—was no more than six hundred yards.

Le Chêne was a charming rural bar nestled between fields on the road leading from La Lande to the junction with the departmental road and facing the entrance road to Greno. Four varnished Bordeaux barrels with black strapping adorned the stone terrace and a man was standing by one of them, smoking and sipping a glass of muscadet. Voices could be heard coming from the other side of the green door which had been left ajar. Beside it was a huge basket full of pumpkins, and the cardboard sign squeezed between the basket and the whitewashed wall read: *Citrouilles d'Halloween 3€.* The building's thatched roof was covered in moss and towering behind it was the magnificent oak in whose honour the bar had been named.

They pushed their bicycles around the back and leaned them against the oak.

'Arnaud always beats us here,' Youna remarked quietly to Rowan.

'It's his Saturday morning ritual. He gets a few minutes to himself in the morning and Nina gets some time for herself in the afternoon.'

'That's not a bad idea. We should do that once we're married with children.'

'I think I'm going to need a drink before I get drawn into this conversation,' Rowan replied.

She laughed.

'Morning, ladies. Rowan,' Arnaud said.

'Got yourself a nice spot in the sun there,' Rowan said.

'I need to warm up after the storm last night.'

'Definitely. Keep you up, did it?'

'Not on your life. I sleep like a log. Bad weather's my lullaby.'

'Busy inside?' Louane asked.

'Not really. Kevin and his hairy girls aren't here yet.' He laughed. 'Thérèse has just arrived. She might have some eggs left if you're interested. Those pumpkins are from her garden. She's getting more into the Halloween spirit every year. The kids can't wait for next weekend. You lot dressing up?'

They looked at each other. 'We haven't thought about it,' Gwen said. 'We should.'

'We'll be staying in Greno,' Arnaud said. 'Feel free to drop by our place if you go trick or treating.'

'Thanks,' Rowan said. 'Excuse us while we grab a drink.'

'By all means. I'm heading off in a minute. Say hello to your dad for me, Rowan.'

'Will do.'

They stepped inside and were greeted by Hervé Guivarc'h behind the bar and Thérèse Derrien standing by a stool on which sat her basket of eggs. Hervé lived with his mother in the house next to Madame Derrien's. His mother worked at a supermarket in Herbignac and helped her elderly neighbour with her shopping, even throwing in a free product or two whenever possible.

'What can I get you?' Hervé asked, looking Louane up and down with his pale blue eyes as he spoke.

'A pint of La Morgane for me,' Rowan said.

'Same for me,' Youna said.

'Got a bottle of sparkling open?' Gwen asked.

'There's a nice Vouvray.'

'Make it two,' Louane said.

'With pleasure.'

Louane looked at Gwen and rolled her eyes. Although not bad-looking, Hervé was a bit rough around the edges with his unkempt hair and dirt under his fingernails, and he tended to lay it on a bit thick considering he knew she was spoken for. Not her type at all. All the same, the attention flattered her.

'You young folks need any eggs?' Thérèse asked. 'I have more than enough. I'd ask your father, Rowan, only he hardly ever leaves the house.'

'Working on another book, no doubt,' Hervé added flatly.

'Same old story,' Rowan replied. 'I've got plenty. Thank you, Thérèse.'

'Ladies?'

'Not today. Thanks.'

Hervé passed them their drinks. 'I saw Fred cleaning up around your place this morning.'

'That's right,' Rowan answered.

'He's still doing gardening for your dad then?'

'Yeah, why wouldn't he?'

'No reason.' Hervé shrugged. 'He told me he had a lot on his hands at the moment. That's all.'

'He didn't say anything about it to me this morning.'

Hervé nodded.

A current of air filled the bar as the door opened.

'There you are, Kevin,' Hervé said with a smile. 'The usual outside?'

'You got it. Fred not here?'

'He's doing the gardening at Ker Greno.'

'Of course. I'll catch up with him later. You here all day?'

'The landlord's supposed to be taking over at lunchtime. I'll be behind the bar again for happy hour.'

Kevin looked around, said hello to the others, and told Hervé to join him outside for a smoke when he was ready.

'Let's go out to the terrace,' Youna said. 'We need to soak up the sunshine while it lasts. This is the last weekend before Halloween heralds the beginning of the black month.'

'The black month?' Gwen asked.

'You haven't been hanging around Rowan's dad enough,' Youna said. 'Professor Trevelyan can tell you all about it. November is *miz Du* in Breton—the black month.'

'In that case, let's make the most of it before darkness engulfs us all—to the terrace!' Gwen declared and headed for the door.

4. Horse and Cart

Gwen chose the barrel where Arnaud had been. She sat on a stool and closed her eyes as she turned her face to the sun. Rowan grabbed a spare stool from the barrel Kevin was at so they all had one.

They clinked their glasses to a chorus of *santés* and *yec'hed mats*.

'Really hits the spot, doesn't it?' Kevin said.

They raised their glasses to him and nodded.

'Nothing like a cold beer after a nice ride.'

Louane managed to contain her laugh, but a fine spray of Vouvray escaped her lips all the same. Rowan ignored her but he caught the fleeting smirk on Kevin's lips.

Just then, Ruby and Cayenne sat up straight and looked along the road to La Lande. Everyone noticed and did the same. A pleasant clopping sound reached their ears and a dark-haired teenage girl came into view, towering over a hedge of gorse. Seconds later, they saw the horse—perfectly black except for a thin white strip like a slither of moonlight stretching from below the forelock almost to the muzzle. The girl's poise bore witness to her experience as a rider and before she made her steed turn—the gesture or word unnoticed by the spectators—she raised a hand to touch the brim of her riding hat. Rowan didn't fail to notice that there was no accompanying smile whatsoever. She turned her attention back to where she was heading and the horse broke into a trot.

No one spoke until she was out of sight.

'Magnificent creature,' Kevin remarked, still looking that way.

Rowan waited for a hint of innuendo from Louane or Gwen, but none came. Perhaps they drew the line at suggesting a man more than twice the girl's age might be indulging in inappropriate thoughts.

'He certainly is,' Rowan agreed.

Kevin guffawed. 'You know as much about horses as my ex says I do about women. That's a mare.'

Rowan shrugged. 'Whoops.'

'Don't worry. You've got your priorities right.'

Hervé joined them on the terrace. He sat next to Kevin and passed him a cigarette.

'Quite the storm last night,' Kevin said.

'It was—made a mess of the garden. I've promised my mum I'll clean up tomorrow.'

Rowan discreetly listened in on their conversation while the women started their own. He was eager to find out whether Kevin would mention last night's less natural disturbance, but the conversation veered quickly from gardens and vegetables to the cost of living and fuel prices more specifically.

'Are you staying over tonight, Rowan?' Youna asked hopefully.

'If I'm invited.'

He couldn't tell them he was in two minds about it and that he didn't want to leave his father alone for too long.

'Of course,' Louane said.

'Always,' Gwen added.

'Let's play it by ear,' he said.

'We could have raclette,' Gwen said. 'We have everything we need.'

The others agreed.

Thérèse left the bar and bid everyone farewell but she stopped in her tracks before leaving the terrace and turned around.

Noticing the vaguely troubled look on her face, Kevin asked her if she was feeling unwell.

'Oh no,' she said with a faint smile. 'It's just that, you all know I'm happy to share my eggs and vegetables with you young folk.'

'We know,' Hervé replied. 'It's very kind of you.'

'Yes,' she said hesitantly.

'What's wrong?' Hervé asked.

She studied their faces, and Rowan and Youna looked at each other, bewildered.

'Nothing at all. I get a little confused in my old age sometimes. I can't even remember what I was saying. Have a lovely day now.'

Hervé and Kevin exchanged a blank glance and shrugged.

'Poor dear,' Kevin said once she was out of earshot.

'It mustn't be easy,' Hervé said. 'Growing old without the one person you love most in the world.'

Kevin gave him a knowing look. 'Your shout, barman?'

Hervé winked at him and turned to the others. 'A round on the house. Same again?'

'We won't say no to that,' Rowan said.

'Didn't think you would. It stays between us though.'

'Loud and clear,' Kevin assured him. 'Our dark little secret.'

They all laughed, and as Hervé went inside, Rowan watched Thérèse make her way slowly down the street into Greno.

#

They left *Le Chêne* shortly before noon when Hervé was obliged to go inside to serve a Parisian couple who appeared to be blissfully lost in the area and Kevin decided to take Ruby and Cayenne for another woodland walk.

Rowan led the way, cruising along the street into Greno with Youna, Louane, and Gwen following in single file. Crows foraged in the fallow field to the left and a Rottweiler barked aggressively from behind the high wire fence to the right. The guard dog had positioned itself between the remains of a Peugeot 106 and a pile of yellow barrier fencing coils ensnared in a tangle of brambles. Rowan had nicknamed this private tip—for want of a more precise term to describe it—*the Eyesore of Greno*. Neither he nor anyone else—as far as he was aware—knew the name of the property's elusive owner, but they were quite certain the man in his late fifties or early sixties was single. He lived alone in a rundown cottage hidden behind an empty grain silo and a workshop made of rusty corrugated-iron sheeting. There was a small stretch of woodland and a field where sheep grazed before the village proper started and well-maintained cottages and gardens lined both sides of the street. A couple of seconds later, Rowan would round the bend and Ker Greno would come into view at the spot where he passed between the old village bread oven and the well.

When his house came into view, he saw Fred standing in the street near the letterbox. The hedge had been trimmed and all the leaves raked up. The gardener was in the process of sticking a wad of twenty-euro notes into the left pocket of his jeans. He was surprised by the sudden disturbance, and not pleasantly so, it seemed to Rowan.

'We need to stop bumping into each other like this,' Rowan joked.

'You haven't seen the end of me quite yet,' was Fred's dry reply. 'Enjoy your ride.'

And with that, he walked past them without a further word, heading to *Le Chêne*.

'What's eating him?' Youna asked.

Rowan watched him walk away and shook his head. 'I really couldn't tell you. He was fine this morning. Dad must have said or done something to put him in a bad mood.'

'He can have that effect on people,' Youna said.

'I'd have thought he was used to it though,' Gwen offered.

'You'd think so, wouldn't you?' Rowan mused, remembering Hervé's question earlier. 'Dad's got a lot on his mind with his new book, and I guess Fred has problems of his own. It's no big deal. They'll sort it out.'

'I guess they will,' Louane chirped. 'Let's get home and have some lunch.'

They started pedalling again but slowed when they turned the corner onto the woodland path to find David and Arnaud standing by the dolmen. Rowan wasn't going to have to say hello to his father on Arnaud's behalf after all. But they hadn't merely exchanged a neighbourly greeting. There was something out of place in the way David's shoulders suddenly relaxed and an ever so slightly exaggerated smile dawned on Arnaud's face. They'd been deep in discussion.

'Hello, David,' Youna said, drawing to a halt.

He returned the greeting, and shot a smile at Louane and Gwen.

'Youna,' Rowan said quietly. 'Go ahead and have lunch without me. I'll join you later.'

'Call me if you change your mind and decide to stay here.'

He looked at his father, who was pretending nothing at all was the matter, before assuring her he'd be there by nightfall.

'Received loud and clear,' Youna said. 'We'll leave you men to your secret business. Do behave yourselves.'

The three women rode off and Gwen frowned suspiciously at the men as she passed them.

Rowan strolled over to the dolmen, contemplated it absently for a moment, and turned to his father and neighbour, who were waiting for him to say his piece.

'What's going on?'

They weren't fooled by the apparent simplicity of the question and Rowan didn't fail to notice the guilty look Arnaud was trying to hide.

'Nina bumped into Jessica Chotard this morning,' Arnaud began. 'You know who I mean—the teenager who rides through here on a black mare?'

'I know,' Rowan said. 'We saw her earlier. She lives on the farm in La Lande. What's happened? Is it to do with her brother?'

'Valentin? No. Well, not directly.' Arnaud gave David a dark look.

Not a soul in La Lande and the surrounding villages would ever forget that day two years ago. A drink too many? A casual disregard for the safety rules? The wrong place at the wrong time? The police investigation had identified several contributing factors and the *procureur* concluded that Valentin's death had been accidental. The hunting party as a whole was found responsible, including Valentin himself and his father, Pascal, the most experienced member. But Pascal Chotard hadn't come to quite the same conclusion. Bruno Garcia never had held his drink quite as well as the others, and the

43

fateful day he shot what he thought was a boar on the other side of the hedgerow wasn't the first he'd been a little too eager to pull the trigger. It was, however, the last. Their hunting licences were cancelled, and in the two years since Valentin's death, the only bloodshed in the area had taken place during boar culls organised by the local authorities.

'There's trouble brewing and I don't like it,' Rowan said.

David laughed it off. 'Don't be dramatic, son.'

'Don't be dramatic? Do you want me to tell Arnaud about your drama?'

'I know,' Arnaud said quietly. 'It was plain enough to see your father wasn't himself. I ended up squeezing it out of him.'

Rowan turned to his father. 'Good. Now, tell me what Jessica told Nina.'

'Her father went into the barn this morning and discovered his antique cart was missing,' David said.

'Is that so?'

'That's what Jessica told Nina.'

Rowan thought about the blank look she'd given them. Thinking about it now, it had been almost cold—no hint of the faintly melancholic smile she usually wore.

'His cart was stolen,' Rowan said slowly, more to himself than to his father or Arnaud.

'In the light of what your father told me about what you both witnessed last night—' Arnaud didn't finish his sentence.

'Their horse wasn't stolen though,' Rowan observed.

'No,' David said, looking from his son to Arnaud. 'That didn't escape our attention. But Minuit wasn't the horse I saw last night. It was a black horse, but I'm certain—one hundred percent certain— that it didn't have a white streak on its forehead.'

No one spoke for a moment and Rowan found himself staring at the dolmen, his mind a muddle.

'It was another horse,' Arnaud said eventually. 'As far as I know, Pascal doesn't have any entirely black horses.'

'Whose is it then?' Rowan asked, not expecting an answer, and nor did he get one.

'He restored that cart with Valentin, not long before the accident,' Arnaud told them. 'Nina has known the family all her life. You know what farming families are like. They don't like to show their emotions too much. But Pascal's wife really opened up to Nina after what happened. She told her that although Pascal found it hard going to the cemetery, he spent time in the barn every day. She'd often find him sitting on the ride-on mower, staring at the cart.

'Who's behind this?' Rowan asked bitterly.

'I can't imagine anyone would want to hurt Pascal,' Arnaud said.

'The thief may not have done it to hurt Pascal, or even know about the cart's significance,' David pointed out.

Arnaud nodded. 'The only person Pascal's ever had a major difference with is Bruno, but he's never forgiven himself for pulling the trigger when he did. I doubt he'd even defend himself if Pascal decided to kill him.'

'Which he nearly did,' Rowan reminded them, remembering the terrible scene at *Le Chêne* the last time either of them had set foot there.

'I don't know what to make of any of it,' David admitted.

'You know more than you're letting on, Dad, and I wish you'd tell me!' Rowan practically hissed.

Arnaud looked around to make sure no one was near.

'What do you think I know, son? I do wish you'd give it a rest.'

'Did you tell Arnaud the horse and cart stopped here at the dolmen?'

'He did,' Arnaud confirmed.

Rowan looked up at his father's bedroom window.

'I didn't see who it was,' David said quietly.

'Do you want to know what Brieg thinks?'

David looked at him straight-faced and Rowan was sure he could tell what was coming.

'I don't need to tell you.'

David shrugged. 'Good. Don't tell me. I'm not interested in what that bum thinks.'

45

'That bum probably knows more about Breton lore than anyone in town except you, Dad.'

David turned to Arnaud and laughed, but the latter saw through the act.

'Did you see the—?'

'Stop it!' David shouted, smothering the dreaded name his son had uttered.

Arnaud took a step back and drew a deep breath.

'Stop it, son! Shut up, son!' Rowan imitated his father. 'You're being a drama queen.'

'Wouldn't you be better off with Youna?' his father asked quietly, and there was an edge of calculated cruelty to the question.

'Yeah!' Rowan spat. 'I would be. I'll leave you to your scribbling, you sad, lonely man.'

'Calm down, both of you, please,' Arnaud said, giving them a conciliatory smile.

'Do you know what he's hiding from me, Arnaud? Just tell me that and not a word more.'

Arnaud shook his head and raised his palms.

'Last chance, Dad,' Rowan said as calmly as he could.

David stuck his chin out stubbornly and kept his lips sealed.

'That's how it's to be?'

David opened his mouth to speak. 'I have to get back to my scribbling.' And with a nod to Arnaud, he walked away.

Rowan stared at Arnaud.

'I don't know what's going on between you and your father, Rowan, and it's none of my business, but if I lay hands on whoever stole Pascal Chotard's cart.'

Rowan didn't dare imagine. As far as he was aware, Arnaud wasn't a violent man, but he was strong and he wasn't one to suffer fools.

'What should I do?' Rowan asked.

'I'm not convinced your father's being completely honest either,' he said lowly. 'If you really think this coachman's stop below his bedroom window was more than mere coincidence—well, I wouldn't leave him alone tonight. Go to your girlfriend's house and have a good time, but come back here to sleep—even if you don't say a word to him. If I still had my old man and had the shadow of a doubt about his safety, I'd want to be there under the same roof with him.'

'Thank you,' Rowan said.

'Get going,' Arnaud ordered him. 'We'll talk tomorrow.'

Rowan looked up at the bedroom window again before riding away.

5. A Case for Oscar Tremont

David Trevelyan spent most of the afternoon alternating between staring at the screen of his laptop and pacing around the library, mostly in a clockwise but every now and then in an anticlockwise direction. Whenever his orbit saw him pass the window that overlooked the public path, he paused and stared beyond the treetops towards where Rowan was in Kergaillot. He went downstairs shortly before two o'clock and fixed himself a tuna and cream cheese sandwich, washed it down with tea, and promptly returned upstairs where he went back to sitting at the computer and writing the odd paragraph or two.

He was running out of time and kept asking himself whether that was his plan. Deep down inside, was he intentionally pushing his blackmailer to the brink—just to find out whether he'd really go through with the threat? The idea thrilled him as much as it terrified him. For the umpteenth time that day, he found himself asking the same question—did people ever act in a truly unpredictable manner? And if it was indeed possible, who could be more unpredictable—David or his blackmailer?

The clock was ticking. Tomorrow was the last day. He'd been reminded of that fact in no uncertain terms that morning. He had to pay in cash by dusk tomorrow. That, in itself, was no longer even feasible. He didn't keep that kind of money in liquid at Ker Greno and the bank was closed. There was no way he could meet the deadline even if he decided to that very instant. Tomorrow, or shortly thereafter, his secret would be revealed.

He walked to the window and contemplated the sunlight brushing the very tips of the treetops, but he saw only darkness.

'Rowan can't know. My children can't know.' His breath fogged the pane. 'It's too late, isn't it?'

He'd procrastinated and now there was no way out—no way except one. The unthinkable. His blackmailer wouldn't think he had it in him. David wasn't convinced himself. After all, it wasn't the kind of act you tried to carry out without being sure you could actually go through with it. You either did it or you didn't. No grey area. No turning back beyond a certain point. If he went ahead with it, he would have brazen unpredictability on his side—but chances were that wouldn't be enough.

The sky grew cloudy before sunset. David had somehow managed to get a reasonable amount of writing done throughout the day, so he went downstairs and poured himself a dram of whisky which he carried with him outside for a quick stroll around the garden. He inspected the hedge yet again and admired the rose buds that would most likely bloom in early November.

As the last lustre of daylight faded, a chill breeze picked up and made him shiver. He looked around the garden, feeling nervous now for no obvious reason, and sipped his whisky. After glancing along the drive to the empty street, he reassured himself that he'd been right to push Rowan away earlier that day. There was truth in the old saying that you sometimes had to be cruel to be kind. His son was better off well away from him, at least for the time being.

David went inside, locked the door, and lit a fire in the wood stove.

#

Brieg shuffled past the dolmen shortly after nightfall. He kept a small torch in the inside left pocket of his coat but didn't use it when walking around the village. There were three reasons for that. Firstly, he knew his way around without it. Secondly, he didn't like to draw attention to himself. And thirdly and most importantly, he wasn't interested in wasting money on batteries. He paused as he reached the end of the path and listened. There was a vehicle arriving in Greno. Looking up the street, he saw its headlights had a yellowish tint to them. Darkness returned as it swung left and the engine died. It was Bruno Garcia in his electrician's van.

An owl hooted nearby and Brieg nodded in agreement as though the bird of the night had imparted a message of profound wisdom. He looked up at Ker Greno for a moment and then walked around to the front of Kevin's cottage. The lights were out and there was no sign of smoke rising into the night sky from the short chimney stack that protruded from the thatched roof. So much for coming over for a drink. He must have walked up to *Le Chêne* for happy hour.

'Bah!' Brieg said to himself.

Another vehicle was coming now. He retreated to the path and sank back against the hedge delineating Kevin's property as the headlights illuminated the twin stone structures of the old oven and well. He recognised Denise Guivarc'h's white Opel Corsa. She must have finished her shift at the supermarket, unless she'd been somewhere else. Perhaps she'd found a boyfriend and had been enjoying herself. Brieg chuckled under his breath, wondering what Hervé would have to say about that. She got out of the car, opened the varnished pine gate her son had recently replaced the old rusted one with, and walked along the brick path to the front door to her cottage. A moment after closing the door behind her, the kitchen light came on and Brieg knew she'd be preparing dinner for when Hervé got back from work. He had to ask himself which was worse, being a hermit in the woods or living at home and having your mother still cook for you at forty-odd years old. But what did Brieg know of mothers? His had spent the latter part of her life in state institutions.

That drink at Kevin's would have to wait for another night. He stroked his goatee and looked at David Trevelyan's bedroom window. There was no light coming from it. Nor was there any coming from the library or either of the other bedrooms. The professor must have been downstairs. But Brieg knew he'd go upstairs later and lie in bed wide awake. That's what he'd do if he was all alone in a big house and believed the Ankou was haunting him—make sure the doors are locked and stay in bed.

He wandered back along the path and into the dark woods. It would be the usual routine—a simple dinner of fried mushrooms, potatoes, and onions with a couple of slices of ham, followed by a cigarette and a few games of patience by candlelight. As far as he was concerned, there was no finer way to spend an evening.

#

A typical Saturday night in Kergaillot was either watching a film or putting a playlist on and dancing around the living room. It depended on what kind of mood everyone was in. Rowan was doing his best to pretend his father wasn't on his mind, but he wasn't fooling anyone—least of all Youna. After their raclette and a scoop of sorbet with a splash of brandy for dessert, Louane suggested they play a game, and asked Rowan to choose.

'How about charades?'

'Oh, we haven't played that in ages,' Gwen said. 'Great idea.'

'You start, Rowan,' Youna told him.

He got up and stood in front of them, waiting for inspiration to strike.

'Ready?' he asked once he'd come up with an idea.

They nodded enthusiastically.

He squatted repeatedly and held his right hand in line with his eyebrow with the thumb and forefinger almost touching.

Youna understood immediately. 'Jessica riding the magnificent creature!'

'Got it!'

Louane and Gwen laughed. 'Your turn, Youna,' Louane said.

Youna swapped places with Rowan and began immediately. She stood facing her sister and looked her up and down, licking her lips.

Rowan burst out laughing. 'Hervé every time Louane enters *Le Chêne.*'

'Hole in one!' Youna said.

'Thanks for that, sis,' Louane said. 'You had to, didn't you?'

51

Youna nodded. 'I'm afraid so.'

'Me again?' Rowan asked.

'The rules are the rules. Get back up there,' Gwen told him.

He decided to stick to the theme he'd started and shuffled around picking invisible items from the floor here and there.

'Brieg harvesting mushrooms!' Gwen shouted. 'An uncanny imitation, by the way!'

Rowan clicked his fingers. 'Thanks, Gwen—I think. You're up.'

The game of charades continued for several rounds and the theme changed from village identities to specific occupations. It wasn't until Gwen's sixth or seventh turn that Rowan realised he'd pushed his father from his mind. She'd been swinging her arms from left to right with her fists at knee height from the floor. Louane had guessed she was playing hockey and Youna had said she was sweeping the floor. Rowan had hesitated before answering, but when he articulated his guess, she nodded.

'Farmer reaping wheat,' he said quietly.

'That's not how you use a scythe!' Louane protested.

'I don't know. I'm not a farmer, am I?' Gwen replied. 'It's just charades.'

'Rowan?' Youna said. 'What's wrong?'

He shook his head, trying to get Brieg's words out of it.

Tell him to be careful it's not the Ankou out for his soul.

A horse and cart passing through the Breton countryside in the middle of the night. What else could it be? He shook his head. But the cart was stolen from Pascal Chotard's barn. None of the legends accused the Grim Reaper of petty theft.

'Rowan?'

He snapped out of it. 'Yes. Sorry. What did you say?'

She was frowning at him. 'You're concerned about your dad, aren't you? I can read you like a book. You've been trying not to think about him all night.'

He nodded guiltily.

'That's normal. It means you care,' she told him.

'Can you call him?' Louane asked. 'Or will he be asleep?'

52

Rowan was sure he wouldn't be—in bed, perhaps, but not asleep. He looked at Youna and she understood. She nodded.

'You don't understand,' he told her.

'I don't understand what's going on with you two, but I understand you're worried. Go home.' She closed her eyes and nodded. 'It's fine, honestly.'

He kissed her. 'I don't know what I'd do without you. I hate him sometimes.'

'Don't say that. You love him, Rowan. He pisses you off, but you don't hate him,' she said softly. 'If you think he needs you to be there tonight, go to him. We've had a wonderful day together. I don't want to be selfish.'

'Youna, is that you or has someone else's spirit possessed you?' Louane asked, and they all laughed.

'I'm impressed,' Gwen said. 'You heard her, boy, get out of here. You'll be with her in her dreams tonight—and maybe ours too.' She winked at her cousin. 'But seriously, take it from a girl who had a really messed-up relationship with her dad. If it's not beyond fixing, fix it!'

'Thank you,' Rowan said. 'You're right.'

He bid them all good night, kissed Youna again, and put his jacket and shoes on.

A gentle but chill breeze accompanied Rowan on his way out of Kergaillot. It was after midnight and there were only lights on behind the curtains of a handful of the houses that didn't have their shutters closed. He checked his phone. No message from his father. Not a single one. But that wasn't unexpected. David Trevelyan was averse to using his smartphone at the best of times. He claimed they stifled clear and critical thinking and led invariably to poor writing. Putting his phone in one of his jacket pockets and removing a small torch from the other, he told himself—not for the first time—that the man was a bit of a hypocrite. The manner in which he'd told his son he didn't want him around hardly made him the epitome of eloquence. He had a habit of keeping all his fine words and turns of phrases for his writing.

Rowan glimpsed the moon whenever a gap in the cloud cover appeared.

'Waning gibbous moon,' he whispered to himself and watched the fog rise from his mouth.

For every failing his father had, there was a compensating strength, and foremost among them was the wealth of general knowledge he bestowed on his son.

Rowan pulled the hood of his jacket over his head as he passed the last house before the woods and switched his torch on. Every now and then, he heard the ping of an acorn hitting the leaves below. That was where the hood came in particularly useful. Taking an acorn from the highest branches of an oak tree on the bare head was an unpleasant experience. But Rowan reminded himself that a falling acorn wasn't his greatest concern if indeed the Ankou was roaming the countryside.

He shook his head. *If the Ankou was roaming the countryside?* He had to put a stop to these crazy thoughts, and yet, there were so many warning signs. Brieg must have seen some of his own. No one was more observant than him. He had time on his hands, and he never stopped rummaging. He noticed details others ignored. Rowan's father, for all his analytical thinking, had been spooked. He was hiding something from his son. Then there was the stolen cart. And tonight—surely by pure coincidence, or simply because it was the harvest season and she'd seen combines at work in the fields— Gwen had performed an impression, however poor it may have been, of a reaper.

He stopped in his tracks. He'd heard a noise. One that didn't belong to the woods. He lowered his hood to hear better and held his breath. Nothing. Certainly no hammering hooves or grinding wheels. A footstep? But he was still some distance from Brieg's caravan, and he wouldn't be out and about at this time of night, especially if he really did believe in the Ankou. All the same, Rowan stayed frozen a little longer, releasing his breath and taking another. Nothing. It had been a squirrel or some other animal landing on a brittle branch. That's what he'd heard. What was a footstep after all, other than the sound of whatever lay underneath being struck? The sound could have been the result of any of a dozen natural causes. He pulled his hood up and started walking again, shining his torch along the path from time to time.

Rowan knew the path intimately and could judge how far along it he was by every slight bend, shallow pothole, and fallen tree. He didn't shine his torch on Brieg's caravan when he passed it. That wouldn't have achieved anything except running the risk of unnecessarily disturbing the hermit. He knew precisely where it was and that he would reach Ker Greno within a couple of minutes.

When the grand house came into view, he immediately saw that the upstairs lights were off. He supposed his father was lying awake in bed, but an almost imperceptible movement behind the bedroom window put a sudden end to that assumption. It was little more than a shifting shadow, but it was enough to know David Trevelyan was out of bed and on edge. Then, as he drew nearer, Rowan saw the profile of his father's face, but it was obscured a moment later when he raised his hands to his face. There was a pinpoint of red light. It could only be one thing—a camera—and that meant—!

Rowan's gaze dropped to where the camera was pointed, and he gasped audibly at what he saw. In front of the dolmen, no more than a hundred feet further along the path, a figure dressed entirely in black—hat with buckle, coachman's gloves, and all—stood in a cart attached to a black horse which was facing him. The spine-chilling skull mask and the curved blade of the scythe being pointed menacingly at the bedroom window glowed in the light emitted from the cart's two lamps.

A wave of fury swelled in Rowan, and without consciously deciding to, he found himself striding towards the Ankou, his torch levelled at it.

'Who are you? Leave my father be!'

The terrifying skull turned to fix Rowan, and although the eye sockets were unfathomable, he could feel the sinister gaze. He regretted his rashness immediately and froze in his tracks.

The Ankou's left hand flicked the reins, and as the horse charged forwards, the right hand raised the scythe high overhead. Rowan was aware of the bedroom window being opened and his father yelling at him to get out of the way, but it wasn't until the horse was almost upon him that he managed to move his body, thrusting himself into the undergrowth of bindweed and nettles by the side of the path. It wasn't until the swinging light from the lamps and the thunderous sound of hammering hooves and grating cartwheels had faded that Rowan understood he'd survived. But the relief was short-lived, and as he hurried to clamber out of the ditch—ignoring the stinging sensation the nettles had left on his face and hands— the wave of anger returned. But this time, it was directed at his father.

Rowan looked at the bedroom window and saw his father gesturing wildly.

'Come inside!' he ordered, barely louder than a whisper, and he blew a long breath through pursed lips as he hurriedly closed the window and retreated out of sight.

Rowan turned to stare into the darkness obscuring the way the Ankou had gone. It was too late and too dangerous to chase the cart through the woods. Instead, using his torch to guide him, he ran around to the drive and up to the door, not even looking to see if any neighbours had witnessed the scene. In any case, no one had stepped out onto the street. He fumbled for his key, opened the door, and rushed upstairs.

David had switched the light on and was standing in the middle of the bedroom, waiting for his son. Rowan shoved the door open, switched his torch off, and glared at his father.

'You need to start talking to me!' Rowan hissed eventually, realising his father wasn't going to speak first.

'Don't be angry at me, son. I beg you. I don't understand either.'

'This is what you saw last night?'

David nodded sheepishly.

'Brieg was right.'

'What do you mean he was right? Don't be ridiculous.'

'It's the Ankou, Dad!'

56

'The Ankou is a folk legend, Rowan. I'm sorry. This is my doing. It's my fault if I've brainwashed you—'

'For crying out loud, Dad. I mean it's someone dressed up as the Ankou, and this is no Halloween prank. This is the second night in a row and that scythe wasn't a plastic prop. I have no doubt about that. You're being targetted.'

'I'm being forewarned,' David said quietly.

Rowan was lost for words.

'Why me?'

'Yes, Dad. Why you? There must be a reason.'

David shook his head.

'I'm calling the police.'

'No, Rowan. You can't. I forbid it.'

'You forbid it?' He narrowed his eyes at his father.

'Promise me you won't call the police.'

'Why? What is it you have to hide?'

David walked to the window and stared at the sky. The moon was hiding behind cloud cover that was growing ever thicker as the night progressed.

'Dad?' Rowan pressed.

He turned from the window. 'It's not about hiding anything. It's about being credible. I can hardly tell the police I'm being hounded by some joker dressed up as mythical being.'

Rowan looked at the camera hanging from his father's neck.

'I saw you taking pictures. Why did you do that if you aren't planning on showing them to the police?'

'I took them for myself, Rowan—and no one else.'

'No one else?'

David closed his eyes.

'He could have killed me tonight, Dad! This maniac could have sliced me open with a scythe! So you need to understand that I don't want to hear you tell me this is none of my business.'

'I'm sorry.'

'Sorry isn't enough. We need to put an end to this before it goes too far.'

David looked his son in the eye but didn't say a word.

Rowan sighed. 'No police?'

'I forbid it!'

'You need to compromise here, Dad,' Rowan said firmly.

'How?' His question was genuine and Rowan knew he had to think fast. There were a number of flaws his father could be accused of having—including outright lying—but he wasn't a man who took breaking his word lightly.

'No police—fine—but we need to find another solution.'

David's face was blank.

Rowan shook his head. He had to come up with an idea.

'We need professional help. We need someone who can shed light on this on our terms.' He looked at his father's camera again and it provided the inspiration. 'We need a private investigator.'

No sooner had the look of sceptical astonishment appeared on the professor's face than it began to fade. Rowan knew he had to keep going.

'I'm sure we can find a reliable investigator who will protect our privacy and discreetly discover what's happening.'

David didn't reply. He just lifted his camera, switched it on, and started studying the photographs he'd taken.

'Can I see, Dad?'

'Of course,' his father said, giving the most reassuring smile he could manage.

Rowan walked over and put an arm around his father, patting his shoulder.

'You're all right, son.'

'Did I hear that right? Did you just give me a compliment?'

'That's enough of that. You heard me. What do you think?'

'I think I'm hallucinating.'

'The shots, Rowan. For goodness sake. What do you think?'

'Oh,' Rowan said, looking at the display screen. 'Can you zoom in on this one?'

David clicked the zoom button a few times and reframed the photo so the mask could be seen.

'Have you ever seen a skeleton mask like that?' David asked.

'No, I haven't. It doesn't look like a cheap plastic one from a pound shop. It's awfully realistic.'

'It looks like a real skull,' David practically whispered, unable to hide the dread in his voice.

'It might be made of plaster.'

'Homemade?'

'It could be, Dad.'

They remained silent for a moment and Rowan felt a shiver run up his spine.

'There's some kind of thin black netting over the eye sockets,' David observed. He zoomed in further, but only the faintest hint of white could be detected behind the material.

'We can't see any part of the person's body,' Rowan said. 'The hands were gloved.'

David groaned. 'This isn't much for a private eye to go on.'

'It's all we have, Dad, and it's better than nothing. This is proof. Zoom in on the scythe for me.'

David scrolled over to the Ankou's weapon, used according to legend to reap souls. This one was clearly authentic. If its cruel blade was as sharp as it looked, it would be capable of removing a human head.

'Professional and discreet, son.'

'Professional and discreet,' Rowan repeated. 'I'll start looking now. You should try to get some sleep.'

David turned the camera off. 'I won't be able to sleep. I'm going downstairs for a whisky. Will you join me?'

'Of course. Pour me a dram while I start looking online for a local investigator.' Rowan took his smartphone from his jacket. 'Professional and discreet.'

David went downstairs and found that Rowan had neglected to close the door when he raced into the house. He closed and locked it, put another log in the wood stove, and poured two generous doses of whisky.

Rowan arrived downstairs a moment later and curled up on the sofa. His father passed him his glass and they said cheers with a good deal more heart than usual.

Little more than a minute later, Rowan looked up from his phone with raised eyebrows.

'What is it?'

'Very impressive.'

'Well, go on,' David said. 'Tell me.'

'There happens to be a local detective with an excellent track record.' Rowan watched his father closely. 'Reviews praise him for—among many other qualities—his discretion.'

'I wonder if hunting down supernatural beings is part of his repertoire.'

'He specialises in cases outside the scope and beyond the competence of the police.'

David laughed, and Rowan found himself joining in.

'His words?' David asked. 'I like him already.'

Rowan nodded. 'His very own words, and in English.'

'Really? How's that?'

'He hails from Australia originally.'

'You're having me on!'

'I promise you I'm not, Dad.'

Rowan laughed again. It was such a pleasure to see his father's spirits lift and he hoped beyond hope that it would last.

'His name is Oscar Tremont,' Rowan went on. 'Oscar Tremont, Investigator of the Strange and Inexplicable.'

'I'll call him first thing in the morning, even though it's Sunday.' David drained his whisky. 'Another round?'

6. *Bleiz Mor*

Anne prepared herself a mug of coffee, wrapped a blanket around her shoulders, took a folded towel from the foot of the polished stairs, and went up onto the foredeck of the *Bleiz Mor* to soak up the first rays of sunlight. She used the towel to wipe dew off a white wooden deckchair.

Tanguy was still asleep below deck. She smiled to herself. After keeping him up most of the night, he deserved a little sleep-in. While he was only a few years younger than her ex-husband on paper, his appetite and carefree attitude to life—to *her*—made it seem like more than a decade separated the two men. She occasionally missed David's intellectual ramblings, but Tanguy wasn't unintelligent either. He knew everything there was to know about boats and he was terribly clever when it came to entertaining clients and pairing white wines with various fish, crustaceans, and oysters.

Anne enjoyed the aroma of the black coffee while she waited for it to cool down enough to sip it. Another white van entered the historic centre of Vannes through the narrow mediaeval gateway connecting the port with the Rue Saint-Vincent. Merchants were setting up their stands for the Sunday market. From across the port, on the left bank, a jogger was admiring the boat. Tanguy's two-masted schooner was one of the real head-turners in the port. He'd repainted it that summer. The white was now dazzling and the black gunwale distinguished. He'd repaired the decking as well. His grandfather would have been proud to see the *Bleiz Mor* more splendid than she'd ever been.

It was going to be a relatively fine day in Vannes. The cloud cover had moved south-east overnight, heading towards the

Guérande Peninsula—towards where Ker Greno stood hidden between farmland, woodland, and marshland. She thought about Rowan as she tentatively sipped her coffee, trying to remember if he had classes on Monday. She'd ring him later to check and ask if he wanted to have lunch with them. It was still far too early to call. He'd probably spent the night with Youna. Anne told herself there was a chance she'd end up a grandmother sooner than she thought. Alice was busy living the Parisian lifestyle and was in no rush. She hoped Rowan was being careful for the time being—best graduate before starting a family.

A seagull squawked overhead as it descended towards the old town. The party would soon get started for the bird as locals and tourists alike arrived for breakfast by the port before walking through the city gate and up to the marketplace.

She thought about David. She still cared for him, and wished him well. Even if their marriage had turned sour years ago, you don't have two wonderful children with a good man and walk away without a sense of regret for what could have been. She was happy now and she sincerely hoped he was too—she was almost certain he was, in his own way. If not, he was the only obstacle to his own happiness. There was no one else to blame.

Anne heard Tanguy moving below deck. He was putting the kettle on to make himself a coffee. She got up and wiped the dew off his deckchair before repositioning both chairs so they were better placed in line with the morning sun.

'What's this?' Tanguy's deep voice asked as he appeared on the foredeck. 'It looks like the sea washed a mermaid onto our vessel during the night.'

She turned to admire him, already dressed in navy blue Tribord jumper, matching trousers, and white deck shoes. His clear grey eyes admired her in return from under the brim of his Breton cap. In one hand, he carried a mug of coffee. In the other, her phone.

'You don't need to flatter me like a naïve girl, sailor.'

He laughed. 'No, I do not, and there's nothing naïve about you, but I'll carry on doing it all the same.'

'Sit in the sun with me. Did someone call?'

Tanguy sat next to her and handed her the phone. 'Rowan sent a couple of messages just now. I didn't want to pry but I noticed the words *dark secret*.'

Anne gave him a blank look. 'If I'd noticed those words on your phone, I definitely would have pried.'

'If you want to share, that's another story.'

She read the messages.

'Interesting,' she said eventually.

'What does that mean?'

'He wants to know if his dad has any dark secrets he should be aware of.'

It was Tanguy's turn to look at her blankly. 'And?'

'You know,' she began. 'I've always assumed he did.'

'But you don't know for sure?'

She shook her head and took a long sip. 'No.'

'Why is he asking this now, barely after the crack of dawn on a Sunday morning?'

'Good question.'

'Something's occurred to you. I can tell.'

Anne took a deep breath and closed her eyes as she turned her face to the sun. A moment later, she opened her eyes and turned back to Tanguy.

'You're right. You know your mermaid well. I'm not sure it exactly qualifies as a dark secret, but he was definitely secretive during one of the episodes that ultimately led to me leaving him.'

'Go on.'

'At the time, he and another man from the village were on the hunt for treasure hidden during the French Revolution or the German Occupation. Both were historic periods when wealthy landowners had to find a safe hidey-hole for their money, gems, and heirlooms.'

'And many of them never lived to retrieve their treasure, and had failed to leave clear instructions for their descendants to follow,' Tanguy said.

'Quite so. Anyway, he changed,' Anne said sadly. 'His passion for history and tradition was one of the reasons I was attracted to him in the first place. He was different—this charming young Cornish man who could hardly speak French. So mysterious. He'd say a few words to the older Bretons in Cornish and they'd understand most of what he said. I was the one who felt like a foreigner.' She laughed. 'He changed with time, and the passion became obsession. There were nights I felt like he'd completely forgotten he was married at all. But I've told you all this over and over again, Tanguy.'

'You have, but you've never mentioned a secret.'

She stood and wandered to the bow. He followed her. Together, they stared into the water.

'They found a treasure. I'm convinced of it.'

'But they didn't declare it?'

'No. I guess they wanted to keep it for themselves.'

'Did David know you were planning to divorce him at this time?'

'Not at all. I hadn't made my mind up yet. I kept giving him chances to change.' She paused. 'It wasn't about keeping money from me. He wasn't like that.'

'Has he broached the topic—his partner?'

'We never saw him again. Rumour has it he ran off on his wife. They say he had a lover.'

'Everyone knew about the treasure hunt?'

'It was common knowledge, of course, but David told us they never found the fabled treasure they were after around the ruins of Ranrouët Castle.'

'This other fellow's disappearance, however, made tongues wag,' Tanguy suggested.

'Did it ever!' Anne said, turning her gaze from the water to him.

'I wonder if this is what Rowan has on his mind.'

'There's only one way to find out,' Anne replied, and she entered the code in her phone and called her son.

#

64

Rowan was jogging along the woodland path when his mother called. Despite the terrifying encounter last night, he needed to get out and clear his head before calling the private investigator, and he needed to talk to his mother without any chance of his father overhearing. David hadn't emerged from his bedroom before Rowan left, and he hadn't been standing at the window when Rowan thoroughly examined the dolmen and the ground around it. Presumably, when the combination of fatigue and whisky had finally taken its effect, he'd plunged into a much needed sound sleep.

He stopped to catch his breath and fish his phone out of his tracksuit pocket not far past Brieg's caravan.

'Mum,' he panted.

'Are you all right?'

'Jogging. Give me a second.'

'When you're ready.'

'You got my message?'

'I did,' she said. 'Tell me what's going on.'

'I don't want to worry you.'

'You already have, dear. Is your father behaving strangely—more so than usual?'

Rowan glanced up and down the length of the path. There was no sign of Brieg or Kevin, or anyone else for that matter. Sunday morning was typically dead quiet in Greno—if *typical* still meant a thing.

'It's not so much Dad behaving strangely as someone else, but he's trying to keep it quiet and that's what makes me suspicious.'

'Someone's acting untowardly to your father? Who?'

Rowan explained the situation, and Anne gasped and groaned as she listened.

'Do you think I should go ahead with it?'

'Absolutely,' she said. 'It's a reasonable compromise.'

'But this investigator might dig up whatever it is Dad's worried about being brought to light.'

'So be it,' Anne replied sternly. 'Whoever is haunting him—if that's the appropriate word for this—must have a reason. There has to be an impetus behind it. You're sure no one else in the village has been threatened this way?'

'I'm pretty sure.' He paused. 'Well, to be honest, I don't know. But I've no reason to think so.'

'It sounds personal to me.'

'Why? Does Dad have any secrets?'

'There's no doubt in my mind that he has quite a few. He used to go on treasure hunts. It was more than a decade ago. Do you remember?'

'I do. He was looking for gold hidden during the Revolution.'

'That's right. I'm not sure whether you noticed, but it was a difficult time for us.'

'I noticed, Mum. You know that perfectly well.'

'I'm sorry.'

'There's no need for that. I know you are,' he said. 'But I don't understand how that could be connected to what's going on now. It was ten years ago and Dad didn't find any treasure.'

'How do you know that?'

Rowan was speechless.

'Well, I mean, neither of you told me he did.'

Anne laughed, and Rowan could hear both sweet and bitter notes in there.

'Rowan,' she said softly. 'Your faith in your father's openness isn't completely broken, and that's beautiful—'

'But?' he said.

'Exactly—but it probably won't last much longer. He loves you, and he loves your sister, but he also loves his secrets.'

'What are you saying?'

'I'm not saying anything. He may very well have discovered an important treasure, or all his hunts may have been fruitless. I can't tell you that, because he wouldn't have told me. That's what I'm saying.'

'I'll confront him on the topic,' Rowan told her firmly. 'I'll make him tell me.'

He knew his mother, and he knew her silence was negation.

66

'Mum?'

'Listen to me, Rowan. Let this investigator do his job. If he's worth his salt, he'll dig up everyone's dirty little secrets, including yours.'

Rowan laughed. 'I don't have any, Mum.'

'That's disappointing, dear.' She laughed. 'I'm joking, of course. You're still young—plenty of time to weave webs of your own. Was your father asleep when you left the house?'

'I think so. I didn't see him.'

'This investigator—'

'Yes?'

'I was thinking maybe you could call him today. Do you see what I mean?'

'Have a word with him on my own before he talks to Dad?'

'Why not? It was your idea to hire him after all.'

'I'll do that. I'll call him now.'

'By the way, are you coming to Vannes tomorrow?'

'I don't have any lectures. I haven't decided.'

'Either way, can you call me this evening to keep me informed?'

'Of course, Mum. Say hi to Tanguy for me.'

'He's here. He says hello back. How about your Youna? Looking after each other?'

'We are.'

'Good. I love you, Rowan.'

'Love you, Mum.'

Rowan ended the call, looked up and down the path once again to make sure he was alone, and then opened his phone's internet browser and went to Oscar Tremont's website.

7. Oscar Enters the Scene

Oscar Tremont was about to don his gardening gloves when his phone rang. It was an unknown number. He dropped his gloves by the back door and answered the call.

'Oscar Tremont.'

'Good morning. My name is Rowan Trevelyan. I'm terribly sorry to disturb you on a Sunday morning.'

'Good morning to you, Mister Trevelyan, and I beg you not to apologise. Judging by your fluent English with only the slightest hint of a Gallic accent, coupled with your family name, I'd venture that your father is of Cornish descent but that you've lived all or most of your thirty-odd years here.'

Rowan was taken aback, and his silence made Oscar smile contentedly.

'That is rather impressive!'

'Simple deduction—Sunday morning games if you like. How can I be of service?'

'Your website says you investigate mysteries too, what's the word—?'

'Strange?' Oscar helped him.

'Yes,' Rowan said. 'Too strange for the police.'

'That's what I do. I tackle cases that are out of their realm of expertise or beyond their reach, and I'm not tangled up in as much red tape.'

'Is there a limit to the level of strangeness you can handle?'

Oscar thought it was a shame the young man couldn't see his wicked grin and twitching moustache.

'There is no limit. What is the general nature of the mystery?'

'My father is being haunted by someone dressed up as the grim reaper according to the Breton tradition.'

'My word! You mean to say the Ankou rides?' Oscar exclaimed, and he grinned again at his interlocutor's stunned silence.

'I—' Rowan couldn't gather his words.

'I'm not big on phone conversations, Rowan. Can I call you by your first name?'

'Please do.'

'Likewise for you. As I was saying—not big on faceless chats. What do you say we continue our discussion in person at your earliest convenience?'

'Whenever you're ready.'

Oscar surveyed his garden. Autumn had set in and there was plenty of tidying up to do, but it could wait a few days if need be. Louise and the boys were inside, starting the day slowly.

'I'm ready now. Where do you live?'

'In the village of Greno, not far from Guérande. Are you familiar with the area?'

'To some extent. It's on the road to Herbignac—the one that begins at the Devil's Windmill in Guérande?'

'That's right. You have to turn off the road about halfway along.'

'There's a nice little bar, isn't there? It's an old whitewashed cottage.'

'*Le Chêne*,' Rowan confirmed. 'You turn right there and follow the street into Greno. We live in Ker Greno. It's the manor on the right-hand side at the end. You can't miss it.'

'I'll be there within the hour. Depending on the particulars of the case, and assuming all parties agree to the terms, I may need to stay one or several nights.'

'We have spare rooms.'

'Your father is aware you've contacted me?'

'He is,' Rowan replied matter-of-factly.

'I sense you're not telling me everything. Is he in favour of engaging my services or are you my client?'

'He begrudgingly accepted. He didn't want to get the police involved but conceded to my suggestion of hiring a private

69

investigator.'

'I see,' Oscar said.

'As it happens, I suspect he may know more about these goings-on than he's letting on.'

'I must tell you, Rowan, that this is generally the case. There's no doubt about it. Whether he is aware of the connection or not, however, is a different matter. Rest assured, if I do take your case, I will explore all avenues of investigation. Naturally, you need to appreciate that I can't guarantee the findings will be to your liking.'

'I understand that. I've already considered that possibility. It's a risk that has to be taken.'

'That's clear then,' Oscar said. 'I'm as good as on my way to Ker Greno.'

'Thank you.'

With that, Oscar Tremont went back inside the house, let his wife know what was happening, and started gathering the tools of his trade. Experience had taught him you never knew what might come in handy once the game was afoot.

He kissed Louise and gave his sons a playful punch to the arm before leaving the house and climbing behind the wheel of his vintage Peugeot 403. He'd washed her the previous morning and the black paintwork glistened under the soft sunlight that somehow managed to pierce the cloud cover.

Starting her up, Oscar checked the rear-view mirror even though he wasn't yet ready to pull out. It was somewhat of a habit he'd developed over the years since first setting himself up as a private investigator back home in Australia in his late twenties. It wasn't really a matter of thinking anyone was keeping tabs on him. As far as he knew, he'd never been tailed in Brittany—the last time he was aware of that happening was when he was on the hunt for the lost fortune belonging to the Stayne family in Brisbane. Nevertheless, Oscar rarely failed to take a quick glance along the length of the street behind him before driving off.

Not a soul appeared in the mirror and there was no sign of movement along the street in front of him either. He flicked the windscreen wipers on to get a clearer view. If there had been a thin layer of morning frost, it had already melted. Further along the street, a dog on the roam appeared from around the corner and sniffed around the base of a public bin.

Oscar turned the radio on and listened to the sensual voice of the announcer introducing a new recording by a Bulgarian folk music group. That would do nicely. He pulled his jacket hood up around his neck and flipped the Scottish flat cap he'd left on the passenger seat onto his shaved head. The Peugeot oozed old-world charm but lacked modern comforts like effective heating. These were mere details to Oscar—small sacrifices to make when one owned such a magnificent vehicle.

He checked for traffic this time and pulled out once a silver Mercedes with a Morbihan licence plate had passed. The drive out of town and along the motorway to Guérande was quiet, and once he'd reached the road to Herbignac, there were more cyclists and tractors than cars. The music alternated between folk, blues, and prog rock, and while he listened, Oscar wondered what in the world—or beyond it—could have possessed a flesh-and-blood human being to dress up as a figure from Breton legend and plague a fellow man. Because experience had taught him that however bizarre the case, there was one unfailing certainty—the solution never involved ghosts and ghouls, or curses and spells. The mysteries he tackled were often—but not often enough for his liking—extraordinary, but not one had yet proven to stem from supernatural causes.

He carefully overtook a tractor and turned left onto the road to La Lande a minute later. He proceeded slowly now, taking in the scenery around him—the trees, the fields, the empty terrace of *Le Chêne*—because experience had also taught him that the key to a case was often provided at the very beginning, but without context it could so easily be overlooked. Turning right to enter Greno, he noted the junkyard and hoped the key wasn't in there. When he entered the village, two women he'd soon learn were Thérèse Derrien and Denise Guivarc'h stopped chatting to observe him with open curiosity for a second before turning back to each other and pretending the topic of conversation hadn't changed.

He slowed to a stop between the oven and the well, looked the grand abode to his right up and down, and continued along the drive. He parked by the salt cedar and noticed the silhouettes of two men through the kitchen window. His attention then went to the wooden double garage with slate roof at the far end of the building. There was an impeccable white Land Rover and a dusty grey Volkswagen Polo. No other vehicles. First impressions announced father and son living alone in a spacious manor.

David and Rowan came outside to greet Oscar as he got out of his car.

'Mister Tremont,' David said in a businesslike manner as he strode over, hand extended.

'Good morning, Mister Trevelyan,' Oscar replied. 'What an absolutely magnificent home you have!'

'Very kind of you. Welcome to Ker Greno.'

'Nice to meet you, Rowan,' Oscar said.

'Thank you for coming so quickly,' Rowan replied.

'Not at all.' He turned to David. 'As I discussed on the phone with Rowan, I assure you I'll treat your case with the utmost tact and discretion if I agree to accept it.'

'Good show,' David said. 'Very good. It's not the kind of tomfoolery one wants to have made too public. I can't imagine what's behind it all.'

Oscar narrowed his eyes almost imperceptibly but smiled jovially. 'We'll get to that. First things first.'

'Quite so,' David agreed. 'Tea or coffee?'

'Do you have herbal tea?'

'I think so—mint tea perhaps.'

'That would be just fine.'

'Follow me.'

They entered the house and David told Oscar and Rowan to take a seat in the living area while he put the kettle on.

'My son has filled you in on the details?'

'Not entirely. I thought it best to come to see you both in person. Can you describe the—er, well, the Ankou?' Oscar asked, looking directly at the camera sitting on the coffee table.

'We can do better than that, can't we, Dad?' Rowan asked, making sure one last time that it was his father who gave the green light.

David remained stone-faced as he poured boiling water into their mugs. 'Show him,' he said eventually.

Rowan turned the camera on and showed Oscar, who promptly frowned. 'This certainly is troubling, to say the least. The costume appears accurate in every detail, and the scythe—' He glanced meaningfully at David as he sat down and placed the mugs on the coffee table.

'It's real. It has to be.'

Oscar stroked his moustache and bit his bottom lip.

'You did well to contact me.'

'My father is an expert on Breton and Cornish legends,' Rowan said.

Oscar nodded. 'I thought I recognised the name. I have one of your books at home, though I must admit I haven't picked it up in quite a while. You've never had any particularly unpleasant runs-ins in the world of academia, Mister Trevelyan?'

'Please, do call me David,' he said. 'What exactly do you mean by run-ins?'

'Disputes over copyright or contracts—that kind of thing?'

David thought about it but ended up shaking his head.

'I put it to you that if this person has dressed up as the Ankou and paid so much attention to detail—the horse and cart, the terrifying costume, the all-too-real scythe—and has threatened you—an expert on Breton lore—and no one else—' Oscar cut himself short and shrugged.

'There's no coincidence,' David finished for him.

'None at all. Now, what we don't know is why you're being spooked in this way and what the perpetrator hopes to achieve.'

'Dad?' Rowan asked.

David thought about his blackmailer, but that didn't make sense. He wondered whether it was better to tell Oscar upfront or wait and see whether he'd find out. If it had nothing to do with what was happening, there was no reason to mention it. Either way, today being the deadline, his secret would likely be known to all by sunset tomorrow. He decided to keep quiet.

'I don't know, Rowan. I've told you I don't know what's going on. I hope this isn't merely some prank. Halloween is only a week away.'

Oscar sipped his mint tea. 'Is it common in the village for people to ride around in the middle of the night dressed in a faultless Ankou costume and brandishing a scythe a week before Halloween?'

'No,' David muttered. 'It is not.'

'I didn't think so. These pictures were taken last night?'

They nodded.

'Rowan, you mentioned this having happened more than once.'

Rowan gave Oscar a full account of everything that had happened between when he fell asleep watching *Vera* and his encounter with the Ankou.

'Did he forget to mention anything, David?'

'No. That's the sum of it.'

'I'll need to speak to this farmer.'

'We can arrange that,' David said.

'Has he reported the theft to the police?'

'I don't know. I doubt it. It almost certainly wasn't covered by insurance and he doesn't have much faith in them.'

'I can appreciate his reticence. There's always a chance the thief left a clue at the scene. I'd like to visit him today.'

'Understood,' David said. 'We'll do that.'

'Wait,' Oscar said and sipped his tea.

David and Rowan looked at him and then exchanged a glance.

'Wait for what?' David asked.

'Don't contact him yet,' Oscar said. 'Have you told anyone else about my presence here?'

'Not a soul,' David assured him.

'No,' Rowan said. 'Oh—I told my mother.'

'What?' David almost shouted.

'I spoke to her this morning,' he admitted.

'You didn't ask me, son.'

'She's my mother,' Rowan said sternly. 'I talk to her all the time and we tell each other what's happening in our lives.'

David didn't reply.

'She doesn't live in town?' Oscar asked.

'She lives in Vannes.'

'Good,' Oscar said. 'That's fine then. Does she regularly communicate with anyone else here in Greno?'

Rowan shook his head.

'Right,' Oscar went on. 'The Ankou has made an appearance two nights in a row. We will work on the assumption that he will come again tonight. No one must know I'm here. I'll park my car somewhere hidden away and stay indoors all day. It must look as though your routine has remained undisturbed. Understood?'

They nodded.

'In the meantime, we do nothing?' Rowan asked.

'I wouldn't say that. For a start, I wouldn't mind a tour of Ker Greno. In particular, I need to see your bedroom, David. For purely professional reasons, of course. I'm a happily married man.'

They laughed.

'As a matter of fact, I'll need to commandeer your bedroom for the night. You don't mind sleeping in another room?'

'I see. You want a front-row seat. By all means. Be my guest.'

Oscar finished his tea, looked all around the living area and kitchen, and got to his feet. The first step to solving a mystery of this nature, which was essentially the planned persecution—or "haunting"—of a particular target, was to investigate the receiving end. It was much more difficult to identify the perpetrator without any notion of motive or without establishing a causal link between the two parties.

'How many people live in the village?' he asked.

'I'd wager no more than twenty or thirty,' David answered with a shrug.

'Twenty adults—tops,' Rowan said. 'You think it's someone from here?'

'I don't think anything yet. Groundless guesswork isn't part of my job description. On the other hand, understanding patterns and logistical restrictions is.'

Oscar walked around the living area, looking everywhere as though trying to find car keys.

'Who knows how to ride a horse around here?' he asked.

David and Rowan looked at each other.

'More or less everyone,' Rowan said.

'That's what I thought,' Oscar replied. 'Mind you, harnessing a horse to a cart and keeping control while handling a scythe is a different kettle of fish.'

'Granted,' David said.

'How many names spring to mind now?'

Rowan thought about it before answering. 'It's hard to say. The name of just about every man in the village still comes to mind as being potentially capable of such a feat, plus a few from further afield.'

'Quite so,' David added. 'We can't say for certain who could manage it. As for the women—Nina makes the list, and Jessica and her mother, of course.'

'Does anyone own a black horse?'

Rowan couldn't help but laugh.

'It's not going to be that easy, is it?' he said. 'Hey, but believe me, the stupid questions have to be asked. I've made the mistake of overlooking them before, only to discover later that a lot of time would've been saved if I'd bothered to ask them.'

'Jessica's horse, Minuit, is the only black one in these parts as far as I'm aware,' Rowan said. 'That's not the one though. She has a white streak on her foreground.'

Oscar nodded and walked over to where he'd left his duffel bag by the door. 'Can we go upstairs now? I'd like to see the view from your bedroom, David.'

David led the way upstairs.

'Impressive suit of armour here!' he exclaimed once he'd reached the top of the staircase.

David turned. 'I'm very proud to be its caretaker.'

'Caretaker,' Oscar repeated. 'I like that attitude. We don't own heritage. We take care of it, and pass it down from generation to generation.'

'I knew we were kindred spirits,' David said. 'I could feel it. I'm glad I let my son talk me into hiring you.'

Oscar examined the complete suit of plate armour and the sword resting in a vertical stand in front of the greaves.

'That means a lot to me,' Oscar said. 'I will do whatever I can to bring this affair to a satisfactory conclusion.'

'This is my room,' David said, opening the door and ushering Oscar in. 'I took the photos you saw from here.' He indicated the window.

Oscar dropped his duffel bag beside the bed and went to the window to look down onto the path and the dolmen. Rowan and David stood there and watched him in silence.

'The path leads through the woods and connects with the next village over?'

'That's right,' Rowan said. 'This is the path I take to see my girlfriend, Youna, in Kergaillot.'

'The Ankou retreated along this path on both nights?'

'Yes,' David replied.

'Did he arrive this way?'

They didn't answer.

'Do you know?'

'Well, no,' Rowan said. 'I didn't see him arrive last night and couldn't tell by the sound the night before. I assumed he came through the village, stopped at the dolmen, and left through the woods.'

'David?' Oscar asked.

'I don't know which way he came. Now you mention it—it did

sound like he arrived from the same way he left last night.'

Oscar nodded. 'That makes sense. Trundling through the village would attract too much attention. It's wide enough down there to turn a two-wheeled cart without too much trouble.'

The sky was a steely grey, threatening rain even though the weather forecast hadn't announced any until Tuesday. Oscar thought he had a tough job, but the poor sods at the bureau of meteorology were dealing in mystery on a whole different level when it came to trying to make heads or tails of the weather in Brittany. He waltzed over to his duffel bag and fished out two small black devices the size and shape of eggs.

'A laser alarm?' Rowan asked.

'Precisely.' Oscar grinned. 'You've seen my car—'

'A real beauty,' David said.

'Thank you. So, you know I'm a bit old school in my tastes. But sometimes you need to cheat a little.'

'You set this up between the house and a tree and when the beam is broken, it sets off an alarm you keep with you here in the room,' Rowan summarised. 'Am I right?'

'Spot on!'

'But a squirrel or bird could set it off,' David said.

'That doesn't matter. I'll rush to the window to check. The main point is that it will wake me up if I happen to nod off.'

Oscar took a pair of binoculars from his bag.

'Like I said, I'd like to keep my presence under wraps for the moment. Rowan, are you willing to act as my eyes and ears?'

'I am,' he replied enthusiastically. 'You want me to put the laser alarm in place?'

'Later,' Oscar said. 'We don't want to risk it being noticed. I'll get you to do that at sunset. What I need you to do now is put your jogging kit on again and go down to the dolmen. Pretend you're using it to do stretches—'

'I've already examined it for clues.'

Oscar couldn't conceal his surprise. 'You have?'

'Naturally. I was out for a run when I called you and I looked all around the dolmen and along the path beforehand.'

'Excellent.' Oscar raised his binoculars to his eyes all the same and surveyed the dolmen and the ground around it. 'Did you look behind it?'

'On it, under it, behind it, all around.'

'No footprints?'

'The ground is too hard. The Ankou was standing on the cart, in any case.'

Oscar lowered the binoculars. 'You can't say for certain that he didn't get off, even for a second.'

'No,' Rowan admitted.

'The stone surface of the dolmen itself?'

'No new scratches or markings.'

'Only lichen,' Oscar mused. 'Listen, Rowan, consider yourself patted on the back.'

'Thank you.'

'I saw scuffs left by the cartwheels.'

'Yes,' Rowan said. 'I noticed them.'

'It's unlikely that will help us much, unless the tracks lead to where the cart is being kept hidden. More likely, they're simply not clear enough or end where I presume the path meets a covered street in Kergaillot.'

'I tried to follow them,' Rowan said.

'You did?' David asked.

'Of course, Dad. There aren't clear tracks. All I know is that the cart couldn't have gone as far as Trébrezan, because there's a muddy stretch too wide to negotiate and it would definitely have left tracks if it had gone through that mud.'

'That's very impressive, young man. What did you say you were studying?'

'Law,' he said with a hint of pride.

'Bloody hell! My fault for asking, I guess. Promise me you'll use it for good, not evil.'

David laughed.

'Who knows, you might save your old man's hide one of these

days!'

David's laugh died.

'Enough of this messing around,' Oscar said, clapping loudly. 'Time to see the rest of this fine home. Are any of the rooms out of bounds?' He turned from father to son, observing their expressions and body language. 'They're the ones I most need to explore.'

'Nowhere is out of bounds,' Rowan answered.

Oscar read David's body language. 'You don't regret hiring me yet?'

'Not yet,' David replied and smiled charmingly.

'Capital!' Oscar exclaimed. 'That's rather boring, mind you, if there are no hidden rooms or secret passages in Ker Greno.'

David raised his palms. 'Sorry to disappoint, my dear fellow.'

There was, however, Oscar noticed, that darting of the eyes again, followed by the ever so slight turning of the back. David wouldn't have even been aware of it.

'In that case, take me where you will.'

'Let's start with the library,' David volunteered, leading the way along the corridor. He opened the door, and waited for Oscar and Rowan to enter.

'Lovely view,' Oscar said, immediately striding over to the window overlooking the drive and garden.

'I suppose,' David admitted.

'You're a gardener, like myself?'

'Afraid not. I have a local chap tend to it for me.'

'This is Fred, is it?' Oscar asked, recalling the names and descriptions of the villagers.

'That's correct,' David replied.

'That round stone structure behind the garage—it looks like a dovecote.'

'It was,' David said. 'It's in ruins, as you can see. I stack my firewood there.'

'Thus the tarpaulin,' Oscar said. 'It would have been three times the height and capped with a conical roof.'

'Yes. Unfortunately, we don't have any illustrations of the original structure. I do have a number of books on Breton architecture and historic estates if that interests you.'

Oscar turned back to David, who was clearly eager to show off his fine collection of books. The man was hiding his fear so very admirably, but Oscar hadn't failed to notice that it had intensified since they'd entered the library and that he kept glancing at the antique shelf clock standing guard over the bookshelf holding a range of bilingual dictionaries.

This little mystery intrigued Oscar as much as it worried him. David Trevelyan's fear had grown more palpable since leaving his bedroom—the room from which he'd seen the Ankou two nights in a row. If anything, it ought to have ebbed.

8. The Dolmen

The sun was setting at a quarter to seven. Its light faded behind the cloudy horizon. Rowan walked casually along the path and looked up at the bedroom window. The light was off but he knew Oscar Tremont was standing there, watching him. When the light flicked on, he smiled. It was Oscar's signal that the laser alarm had worked.

'Well done,' Oscar said when Rowan joined him upstairs.

'What now?'

'The alarm is in place, my car is parked out of sight behind the ruins of the dovecote—all that's left is for us to have a quiet evening together and to keep our heads clear for whatever the night may bring.'

'No whisky then?'

'Very little,' Oscar replied with a wink.

'Do you like salmon?'

'I *love* salmon. You're the culinary member of the household?'

'I am. Mum taught me to cook.'

'You'll need to introduce me to her one of these days.'

'To ask questions about Dad?'

'Would she answer them?'

Rowan's eyes widened and he nodded slowly.

'Good,' Oscar said quietly. 'Let's go downstairs and check on your father now. I need you to help me make sure he follows my instructions.'

'He's forbidden to go outside tonight under any circumstances without your express permission,' Rowan repeated.

'Word for word,' Oscar congratulated him. 'You'll make a hell of a lawyer.'

'We'll see. Oh, and I went to Youna's to borrow a bicycle. It's hidden behind the hedge to the right of the path.'

'I saw. That's perfect.'

Oscar switched the light off and they went downstairs to find David in front of the wood stove. He was adding dry twigs to a pyre he'd built around the burgeoning flame.

'You two have it all under control?' he asked.

'All set to go, David,' Oscar confirmed. 'Your instructions are clear?'

'I'm not a damned child, for crying out loud!' he replied abruptly, then licked a finger he'd let touch the flame.

Rowan offered Oscar an apologetic look, but it was confusion he saw on the investigator's face, not offence.

'I didn't mean to snap like that.' David took two small logs and placed them on the fire.

'There's no need to apologise,' Oscar said warmly. 'You carry a burden that weighs heavy on your mind and we can't truly appreciate what you're going through.'

'All the same, you're right. We summoned you here to get to the bottom of the affair and so I need to follow your instructions to the letter.'

Oscar sat on the sofa and clasped his hands together.

'Thank you, Dad.'

David looked at his son and understood the deeper meaning behind those simple words. He knew that however annoying he might be—however irredeemably stubborn, cantankerous, sceptical, and cagey he was—his son didn't want to lose him.

'That's settled then,' Oscar said quietly. 'The line has been cast and the fisherman's finger awaits the telltale tug.'

'Talking about fish,' Rowan said.

'Salmon was the plan tonight, wasn't it?' David asked his son. 'Does that suit you, Oscar?'

'Was Culhwch given directions in his search for Mabon ap Modron?'

'Brilliant!' David boomed. 'I suspect you'll never cease to astound me, Oscar Tremont.'

83

'And you me, David Trevelyan—and you me.'

The awkward silence that ensued was broken by Rowan's getting up and going to the fridge. 'Since we're waxing lyrical about Welsh mythology, how about leek and jasmine rice with coriander and coconut milk?'

'Your Welshman must be backpacking through Asia,' Oscar quipped. 'That sounds absolutely delicious.'

'I'll pour us all a dram to get started,' David added affably. 'A drop of the Caol Ila?'

'A wee dram to keep my wits about me,' Oscar said. 'With pleasure.'

David stoked the fire a little on his way to the drinks cabinet, and Oscar caught him glance at the longcase clock. It wasn't yet seven o'clock. The Ankou wouldn't make an appearance below the bedroom window for several hours yet, and David would be out of the line of fire in one of the guest rooms.

Rowan stopped chopping leek and came to take one of the crystal glasses his father only brought out for special occasions. They toasted, sniffed the peaty aroma, and drank.

As he savoured the first sip, Oscar stared at the fire, allowing its dance to mesmerise him. The flames licked and twirled but he couldn't interpret their message. He closed his eyes but still saw the fiery ballet. He listened to the crackling and whooshing coming from the wood stove and let it speak to him. The words he heard were written on the pieces of a jigsaw puzzle. He slotted them together.

When Oscar opened his eyes, he saw that Rowan had gone back to preparing dinner and that David was holding his glass up to the fire, watching the light refracted as it passed through the amber liquid.

'That ancient structure—does it have a story?' Oscar asked.

David turned to him but didn't speak at first.

'Go on, Dad. Tell him the legend,' Rowan said.

Oscar saw understanding dawn on his face.

'Oh, the dolmen.' David smiled. 'Legend has it the korrigans built it as a tollbooth of sorts. Both the dolmen and the path through the woods are purportedly prehistoric, and throughout the ages, the korrigans would appear to wanderers to play tricks on them, bestowing gold upon only those who passed their trials and exacting terrible vengeance on any who harmed them.'

'The parallels can't be ignored,' Oscar observed.

'Now you mention it,' Rowan agreed.

'Only I don't think they shook scythes at passers-by,' David said, and sipped his whisky.

'That does indeed amount to more than a mere trick,' Oscar mused, and he sipped his whisky thoughtfully. 'I expect everyone in the village knows this legend?'

'I'd say so,' Rowan answered.

'Full of secrets,' Oscar said.

'Dolmens?' David asked.

Oscar nodded and held his gaze. 'Dolmens—yes. We know so very little about who really built them. We've labelled them the Beaker People, but it's so trite, isn't it? Do you fancy our culture being referred to by future historians as the Tupperware Tribe?'

That got a laugh out of them both.

'Dinner will be ready in twenty minutes,' Rowan informed them.

David opened his mouth to speak but didn't get a word out before the alarm receiver lying next to Oscar sounded. The speed with which he placed his glass on the coffee table and dashed up the stairs left the Trevelyan men flabbergasted. But it only lasted a couple of heartbeats. Rowan raced after him and joined him at the window.

'It can't be the Ankou so early,' Rowan whispered.

'It isn't,' Oscar replied quietly. 'But I'd like to know who it is all the same.'

The last faint glow of daylight reached for the clouds like the feeble hands of drowning ghosts. It was enough to make distinguishing the shadow possible. Someone was shuffling along the path towards the village.

'Is this our hermit?'

'Yes,' Rowan said. 'That's Brieg.'

'Is this part of his daily routine?'

'I'd say so. He spends a good deal of his day wandering through the woods and along the path.'

They watched him pause briefly at the dolmen, appearing to contemplate it.

'He can see in the dark,' Rowan said without taking his eyes off Brieg.

Oscar turned to Rowan. 'It seems so. I wonder whether he can't also see korrigans.'

'Don't tell me you believe these fairy tales?'

Oscar tutted. 'I believe that what others believe matters.'

Rowan took a step back from the window and when Oscar looked down, he saw that Brieg had turned to face them. It was too dim to see his face clearly and to tell whether he was looking up at the window, let along whether he could see them standing there in the dark bedroom. Oscar didn't move and Brieg soon turned left and started shambling back along the path in the direction of the woods.

'That was rather peculiar,' Oscar said, staring at the dolmen. He stroked his moustache.

'He's a weird one,' Rowan said nonchalantly.

'How does he survive?'

'He lives very simply. He rummages around the woods, harvests mushrooms, nuts, and fruit, and he barters with the locals. Now and then, he does odd jobs for cash, cigarettes, and groceries.'

'Does he ever steal?'

Rowan was surprised by the question.

'I'm merely asking.'

'I don't think so,' Rowan said. 'No one in the village has ever accused him of theft.'

'He's appreciated?'

'Well, yes—at worst, you could say, he's tolerated.'

'Your father?'

Rowan shrugged.

'Cool indifference?' Oscar offered.

Rowan smiled. 'Precisely.'

Oscar turned from the window and left the room.

'What are you thinking?' Rowan asked Oscar as they descended the stairs.

'I'm thinking he's the kind of person who sees what others don't—real or otherwise—and that, young man, is very useful.'

'I see.'

'Do you smoke, Rowan?'

'No. You?'

'No,' was all Oscar said.

'Who was it?' David asked. By all appearances, he hadn't left his spot on the sofa.

'Just Brieg,' Rowan said.

'Let me guess—he walked to the dolmen, glanced at the village, and strolled back into the woods?'

'Exactly,' Rowan answered.

'Not exactly,' Oscar reminded him, looking at David.

'Quite right. We got the impression he looked up at the window.'

David frowned. 'Did he see you?'

'The light was off, but it's possible,' Oscar told him.

'I can't imagine Brieg being behind this,' Rowan said.

David nodded. 'Me neither. But then again, I can't begin to think who it could be.'

Oscar sat and looked into the fire as he sipped his whisky.

'What were we talking about?' Rowan asked, returning to the stove to stir the jasmine rice and sprinkle coarse salt over the salmon before putting it in the oven.

'The dolmen,' David said. 'The dolmen and korrigans.'

'So we were,' Rowan said. 'And just as we were talking about it, along comes Brieg on his nocturnal pilgrimage. Uncanny, isn't it?'

No one spoke for a while. The only sounds to be heard were the crackling of the fire, the bubbling of the water on the stove, and the ticking of the longcase clock, which Oscar was quite certain David was making a point of not looking at. Had he noticed that Oscar had noticed?

'There's nothing paranormal about it, son,' David said. 'Our conversation didn't cause Brieg to walk to the dolmen. If anything, it's likely the very opposite.'

'What do you mean by that?' Rowan asked, bringing his empty whisky glass back for the next round.

'I'm confident Oscar perfectly appreciates my meaning,' he replied, pouring his son another dram and motioning for Oscar to take the last sip so he could serve him.

Oscar placed his glass on the coffee table and looked David in the eye. 'Naturally.'

David glanced at his son and shook his head, seeing it still wasn't clear to him. 'Can you enlighten him, Oscar, or shall I?'

'What is the opposite of our conversation causing Brieg to go for a stroll?' Oscar asked.

Rowan was bewildered.

'This isn't a trick question,' Oscar assured him. 'It is, however, more to do with psychology than law. I assure you the answer is as simple as the question. So, tell me, what's the opposite of A causing B?'

Rowan shrugged. 'It's B causing A. If our conversation didn't magically cause Brieg to go to the dolmen—which is obviously the case—then Brieg's going there caused our conversation. But that's equally absurd.'

Oscar met David's gaze again and they smiled smugly at each other. The field of psychology was familiar territory to historians and sociologists. Men like David kept their secrets stowed away in nutshells, and cracking them was no meagre feat.

'It's not absurd at all. You and your father are familiar with Brieg's habits. You know that he often wanders along the path at this time of the evening and that he's prone to stop at the dolmen. Therefore, on a subconscious level, this awareness could very easily have directed the topic of our conversation towards the dolmen.'

Rowan's jaw dropped. 'You're right. It's so simple when you think about it.' He went back to chopping the coriander but stopped and a frown formed on his face. 'Hold on a second. There's a problem with that theory.'

Oscar knew exactly what he was going to say but decided to play along. 'What's that?'

'You brought up the topic of the dolmen yourself without knowing about Brieg's habits.'

'That's a matter of interpretation,' he answered. But he was looking at David, not Rowan.

David pursed his lips, thinking about what to say. He laughed to break the silence and raised his glass. 'Still no regrets, Oscar.'

'Glad to hear it.'

Rowan went back to finely chopping the coriander. He was still frowning.

'Do either of you play chess?' Oscar asked out of the blue.

'We both do,' David said. 'Don't tell me the great investigator of the strange and inexplicable didn't notice my chess set.'

'There was a wooden folding chess set in the library. From memory, it was wedged rather unceremoniously between a tattered copy of *I, Claudius* by the celebrated Robert Graves and a dusty Tibetan singing bowl.'

'Nothing escapes you,' David said.

'Not for long,' Oscar replied.

'That's reassuring. Listen, we'll play a game or two after dinner if you like.'

'With pleasure.'

Rowan set the table and told them to take a seat once the salmon was ready. It was delicious and Oscar wasn't once disturbed by the alarm. No one had walked along the path since Brieg, and if any cats or other animals had ventured that way, they'd been small enough to pass under the invisible beam.

After sorbet and a coffee for dessert, David fetched the chess set from the library, put another log on the fire, and declared the tournament open. The three of them went on to win and lose several games each. The aim, after all, was to spend a pleasant evening together, for no one could predict what the night held in store.

At a quarter past eleven, Oscar decided to turn in.

'This has been a lot of fun, but I think it's time for me to settle in for the night. You both know what you're to do?'

'Follow your lead,' Rowan answered.

'It's your show,' David agreed.

'Wonderful,' Oscar said. 'With that, gentlemen, I bid you a good night.'

He retreated upstairs to prepare for bed, much as he might have done at home, except that instead of putting on his pyjamas, he donned a black tracksuit. After peering out the window, he climbed into bed and left the alarm receiver on the bedside table, next to his camera.

The night was dark and calm. In particular, the lack of wind was advantageous in that it dramatically reduced the risk of a falling leaf breaking the laser beam. Oscar drifted in and out of sleep, and every now and then, he got out of bed and went over to the window, just to be completely certain there wasn't a problem. He'd assumed the Ankou would arrive from the woods, not through the village, but there was always a chance—slim, he told himself—that he was wrong. The noise of the horse and cart had woken both David and Rowan, so it would most likely wake him as well, but all the same, going to the window to check from time to time seemed the most foolproof method of checking the Ankou hadn't slipped through.

On three separate occasions, Oscar noted that the creaking of a floorboard disturbed the nocturnal silence. On one of those occasions, it was followed by the opening of a bedroom door and shuffling along the corridor. The pattern was then repeated in reverse order a minute later. It had probably been David going to the toilet. On the other two occasions, however, there was no indication anyone had ventured into the corridor, thus leading Oscar to surmise he wasn't alone in looking out onto the woodland path from time to time.

By three o'clock, and with no sign of the Ankou, Oscar was beginning to wonder whether he hadn't made a mistake. Had his car been spotted? Or perhaps someone had walked up the drive and heard an unfamiliar voice coming from inside. He remembered Brieg looking up at the bedroom window. Could he have glimpsed the unfamiliar face behind the pane?

Or was there another reason the Ankou had desisted?

Oscar's fitful sleep continued, but he didn't bother going to the window again until the first glimmer of daylight touched the sky shortly after eight o'clock. He stretched his hands over his head, bent his knees, and drew a deep breath. The sky was a magnificent patchwork of azure, orange, and pink. There wasn't yet enough light to make out much at ground level, but Oscar was convinced it hadn't rained.

Rowan was a jogger, Oscar remembered, and nothing would have pleased him more than to join him for a quick run through the woods and marshland. But given the uneventful night, he had to rethink his approach—namely, was he to remain hidden, or was it already too late?

While Oscar gazed at the sky, watching the rich shades slowly but surely yield to the growing white light of day, he considered the steps to be taken. He couldn't tell how long he'd been standing there when he looked back down at the path and the dolmen and was suddenly aware that a change had taken place. He couldn't put his finger on it at first. It hadn't rained—so that wasn't it—and the morning fog wasn't thick.

It was the dolmen itself. He rubbed his eyes and looked again. The arrangement of the stones appeared to have altered.

'Impossible,' he whispered to himself. But he couldn't deny what he saw. Yesterday, it had been a simple dolmen consisting of two upright stones supporting one horizontal slab—the capstone. This morning, there was a fourth stone sitting on top of the capstone. It was small and round—very much like a ball—and Oscar began to wonder whether that was indeed what it was. But no child would have played football along the path in the middle of the night.

There was only one way to know for certain what it was without waiting several minutes more for the daylight to intensify. Oscar took a torch from his duffel bag and opened the window. He switched the torch on, pointed the beam at the object, and immediately stumbled back as though he'd been shoved by an invisible hand.

He sat on the edge of the bed to steady himself and gather his thoughts. Once he could manage to articulate it, one word escaped Oscar's lips—barely more than a sigh.

'Whose?'

9. A Message from the Ankou

The tangle of brown hair fell from the crown of the head and lay splayed on the capstone, making it look as though it had been there for weeks—the hair covering the stone like some vivacious creeper. The eyes were closed. The face was expressionless. It could have been the tumbled head of a neglected statue—except there was no mistaking the hue of human skin for granite, no matter how pale and bloodless it was.

'Like getting blood from a stone,' Oscar heard himself say.

He was sure he'd never forget that image, as under the beam of light from the torch, the rock transmogrified into a severed human head.

But this was no time to wallow. He clapped both hands over his face to make sure he was awake and stood up as straight as an arrow. His mind had suffered a horrifying shock but letting it put him out of action wasn't on the cards. He took his camera from the bedside table and put the strap around his neck, then dug into his duffel bag and pulled out a pair of latex gloves. His objective was to get down to the dolmen and investigate the scene without attracting attention.

But it was not to be so, for no sooner had Oscar opened the bedroom door than he heard movement coming from the next room. David was up and about. He quietly closed the door all the same, and as he turned to tiptoe towards the suit of armour like an overambitious assassin, David emerged from the guest room where he'd spent the night.

'Oscar?' He noticed the latex gloves immediately. 'What's going on?'

'I need you to keep a cool head, David.' He immediately regretted his choice of words.

'I will,' he replied, but his voice betrayed his uncertainty. 'The Ankou didn't call during the night?'

'There was no horse or cart,' Oscar confirmed carefully. 'The alarm wasn't set off. Putting aside the long shot that there was a technical malfunction, no one came along the path from the woods.'

'And yet? Spit it out, man!'

Oscar decided to spit it out as requested.

'David, there's a severed head on the dolmen.'

The expression of absolute horror on his face sent a shiver up Oscar's spine.

'Whose?' he whispered urgently, eager now to make sure he didn't wake Rowan. Then, that awful prospect struck him.

'No,' Oscar assured him, reading the look in his yes. 'It's not your son.'

'I'm good,' David said, and Oscar saw his determination in the set of his jaw and his furrowed brow.

'Stay behind me and don't touch a thing!'

'Loud and clear.'

They proceeded downstairs and put their jackets and shoes on before going outside. The footsteps on the gravel drive sounded unbearably loud in the morning quiet—a pleasant tranquillity that was otherwise disturbed only by birdsong and the motor of a distant tractor. There were patches of blue in the sky, and the sun would soon be high enough to angle its rays over the treetops and onto the thatched roofs of the village. It was this rural comeliness that made the gruesome sight Oscar was about to confront up-close all the more appalling.

David gasped as they approached the dolmen, and when Oscar turned to look at him, he saw all the blood had drained from his face. He raised a hand to cover his mouth, and Oscar hoped he wasn't going to vomit.

'Look at me,' Oscar said firmly, and David obeyed. 'Keep it together.'

David lowered his hand, closed his eyes, and took a deep breath.

'Excellent,' Oscar said, studying his face.

When David opened his eyes again, he glanced from Oscar to the head on the dolmen and back again. Oscar, for his part, didn't take his eyes off David.

'Neither of us was expecting this,' Oscar said.

David shook his head. His jaw was set again and his brow furrowed, but it wasn't the same expression of determination. The look in his eyes—Oscar tried to place it. Horror? Of course. Confusion? Undeniably. But that was just it, wasn't it? It wasn't blunt befuddlement—but confusion of a more acute nature—as though trying to make sense of a situation turned on its head.

'Who is it, David?'

'Fred Gaillo,' he said, with a sense of immense relief.

'Your gardener?'

David nodded and touched his neck as though to ensure his head was still well and truly attached to the rest of his body.

'Why is that a relief?'

'What?' David said, suddenly becoming as rigid as a soldier called to attention.

'Sorry,' Oscar said. 'I guess I misread.'

'No,' David said. 'You're right—I'm just relieved you were right about it not being Rowan.' He turned and looked up at the window of the bedroom where his son had slept, but the light was off and there was no sign of movement.

'That is indeed a relief,' Oscar agreed, looking up and down the path to make sure no one was approaching. 'Listen carefully. I need you to go inside, put the kettle on the boil, and call the police.'

'Put the kettle on the boil?'

Oscar rolled his eyes. 'Yes.'

'Oh, I see,' David said. 'No need to rush.'

Oscar nodded and raised his hands to remind David there was a reason he was wearing latex gloves. 'I'll stay here to secure the area until the police arrive.'

David walked casually back to the house and Oscar jogged to where Rowan had positioned the laser alarm and removed both the emitter and the mirror. This was now a murder investigation. He

95

was going to have to work around the police, but he didn't want them sticking their noses into his methods.

He returned to the dolmen and studied the ground where he was walking as he drew nearer. When his face was as close to Fred's head as he could bear, he examined every detail without touching it. The long hair was damp at the top and matted with blood where it splayed out across the stone, but there was no pool of blood around the head. Dewdrops clung to the forehead, cheeks, and nose. Oscar didn't have the means of calculating the time of death with as much precision as police forensics would, but it was clear that he'd been killed sometime the previous evening and that it hadn't happened here. The cause of death may have been decapitation, or the head may have been sliced off post-mortem. In any case, it had been done cleanly. A sharp scythe? At face value, entirely possible.

What Oscar really wanted to know was why the head had been brought here. Someone had taken the risk of bringing it to the dolmen during the night—from or through the village—and placing it right under David's bedroom window.

He crouched and inspected the ground around the dolmen, but there were no clear shoeprints and no drops of blood. All he found other than dirt and leaves was a single grey feather. He stood up, glanced left and right along the path to check he was still alone, and looked back at the gardener's severed head.

'Why were you reaped, Fred Gaillo?' Oscar asked as he pulled his gloves off.

#

Thérèse Derrien let the curtain fall back into place, then sat herself down at the kitchen table and sipped her coffee. What a peculiar spectacle to witness so early in the day—or at any time, for that matter. She couldn't see the dolmen from her cottage, but there was no question about it—the man wearing a flat cap was the very same she'd seen behind the wheel of a black Peugeot 403 yesterday. She wondered what he was doing at Ker Greno and why he'd been

96

snooping around the dolmen. She'd seen him warily approaching where she knew it stood before retreating along the path, only to come back a moment later, wheeling a bicycle around to the drive. Perhaps he'd lost something while riding along the path and then backtracked on foot to find it. Not his cap, in any case, as he was wearing it. Whether or not he'd found whatever he was looking for, she couldn't say. Either way, he'd obviously renounced his morning ride.

No, but there was more to it than that, wasn't there? Even from a distance, his grave expression had been plain to see. Something was awry.

She put her cup down and walked back to the window. He was coming back now. David and Rowan were with him this time. All three of them were walking around to the dolmen. She couldn't keep her nose out of it any longer. She put her coat and slippers on and opened the front door.

She hadn't even reached the garden gate when the distant sound of sirens on the road to Herbignac reached her ears. That wasn't unusual in the slightest, but when she heard Rowan release a horrendous yelp—jarring and distressing like the howl of an injured dog—she knew the sirens wouldn't remain distant for long.

'What's wrong, David?' she asked.

He strode over and held his hands up to stop her coming any closer. 'Don't look, Thérèse. Stay where you are, please. You don't need to see this.'

'Is someone dead?'

He nodded.

'Near the dolmen?'

'Yes, Thérèse. It's not a pretty sight.'

'Is it murder? Who's dead? Tell me, David. Who is it?'

'Fred,' he said. 'It's Fred Gaillo. He has been killed.'

'Fred? Why would anyone want to hurt Fred? Are you sure it's murder?'

'Thérèse,' he said lowly. 'I'm sorry to be the one to tell you, but you're going to find out sooner or later, and the police are almost here. Fred's head is on the dolmen.'

It looked like she was going to lose her balance, so David put his hands on her shoulders to support her.

'I'm fine, David. I'm a tough old bird.'

He gave her a comforting smile.

'He was beheaded?' she asked.

David nodded.

She took a moment to gather her thoughts. 'How?' she asked eventually, and David understood the question.

'I don't know,' he said. 'I don't know how this could happen in Greno.'

Thérèse looked over David's shoulder. Brieg, Rowan, and this fellow wearing the flat cap were coming over. They all looked suitably stunned and disturbed, but it was immediately apparent to her that Rowan had been hit hardest of all. She put it down to him being the youngest, or simply the most sensitive. It then occurred to her that perhaps he was the only one among them who truly liked Fred, even though she had no reason to think this—especially since Oscar was a stranger. Nevertheless, she was old enough and watched enough current affairs shows on the television to know that murder was more often than not committed by someone known to the victim, and since Fred Gaillo spent most of his time in Greno and the neighbouring villages—she knew there was nothing coincidental about the similarity between his family name and the name of Kergaillot—well, chances were his murderer was very close indeed. It was a sobering thought.

'Rowan,' she said soothingly. 'Do you need a nip of brandy? David, get your boy a stiff drink.'

'I'm fine, Thérèse. Honestly, I'll be all right, but Fred—'

'Who would do such a thing?' she asked, looking at Oscar with what he thought was a hint of suspicion. 'There's been a spot of petty theft in the village recently—carrots have gone missing straight from my garden—but *murder*? Who would kill a decent man like Fred?'

David made a sweeping gesture towards Oscar and was about to attempt an introduction, but he didn't get the chance.

'My name is Oscar Tremont.' He lifted his cap fleetingly and was pleased to note the gesture impressed her. 'It's an honour to meet you despite the circumstances, Madame——?' He pretended not to know her name.

'Derrien,' she admitted after a moment's hesitation.

'I intend to answer both your questions in due course,' he said. 'I beg your patience and indulgence. May I pop in for a cup of herbal tea at your convenience?'

'Well, I suppose so.' She raised her eyebrows and turned to David. 'I'll explain later, Thérèse,' David told her.

The sirens cut out as two dark blue gendarmerie vans with flashing blue lights came into view and David waved them down.

'Gendarmerie Nationale,' announced the young woman who got out of the passenger side of the first vehicle. The passenger of the second vehicle immediately joined her, followed by the drivers.

'Major Faure,' the passenger of the second vehicle said by way of terse introduction. 'A body—a head—has been found?'

'Over here,' David said, motioning for Thérèse to stay where she was and leading the major to the dolmen. The others stayed where they were, getting ready to hold back a crowd of curious villagers as doors started to be cautiously pushed open. The young woman spoke to Thérèse to make sure she was holding up all right.

'Who discovered it?' The major asked.

'That would be me,' Oscar said.

'Name?'

He hesitated, but there was no avoiding it. 'Oscar Tremont.'

The major narrowed his eyes. It didn't always happen, but every now and then, a gendarme or police officer recognised his name.

'Private investigator,' Oscar said, deciding to put him out of his misery. The poor chap was clearly racking his brains.

'Well, well, well,' he replied with a grin. 'I finally get to meet the investigator of the strange and incomprehensible.'

'Inexplicable,' Oscar all but snapped. 'Strange and *inexplicable*. It seems I've underestimated the extent of my fame.'

99

'You're certainly making waves. Tell me, Monsieur Tremont, how did you just happen to be here?'

'I'm assisting this gentleman, David Trevelyan, on a separate matter.'

'Is that so?' The major looked David up and down. 'A separate matter, you say?'

'Yes,' Oscar replied matter-of-factly. 'A private matter.'

'Be that as it may, you'll be required to answer questions when the investigative team arrives.'

'Naturally.'

The major made a kind of muffled grunt and turned his attention to the severed head. He felt his own neck and turned back to Oscar.

'Did you touch the scene?' he asked accusatorily.

'Major! I most certainly did not.'

Major Faure didn't look impressed.

'I secured the scene for you. David, Rowan, and—' He looked around and realised that Brieg had disappeared with the arrival of the gendarmes. 'We secured the scene.'

'The gendarmerie thanks you for it. We'll take over from here. This is not your investigation, Monsieur Tremont.'

'I understand you have your job to do,' Oscar replied. 'I do wonder where the rest of his body is though.'

'*That* is not your concern.'

'Don't you at least want to know who it is?'

The major nodded towards Thérèse, who was showing the policewoman where Fred lived.

'Is Oscar Tremont staying with you?' the major asked David.

'He is,' David confirmed, proudly indicating his home. 'He's staying here at Ker Greno. He saw the head from the bedroom window.'

'I see,' the major said, waving at one of the juniors to get his attention and then gesturing the action he needed him to carry out. 'We're going to cordon off the scene now. Please go back inside and wait for the real investigators to arrive.'

Oscar smiled graciously. He'd come to notice that gendarmes

tended to be somewhat less cocky when he ended up handing culprits to them on a silver platter.

They moved along, and the crime scene was cordoned off.

'Oscar, you didn't, did you?' Rowan asked quietly.

'Didn't do what precisely?'

'You didn't touch—you know—Fred's head?'

'I did not,' he answered. 'I wouldn't tamper with a crime scene.'

David and Rowan studied him but realised he was dead serious.

'I took nothing but photographs.'

They stopped by the well, and David explained what was happening to the neighbours who had emerged from their cottages and gravitated closer.

'What happened?' Nina Moison asked. The children were standing by the front door. She'd obviously told them not to come out until she knew what was going on. 'It's not Arnaud, is it? He went to work this morning. He shouldn't be here.'

'Calm down, Nina,' David said. 'It's not Arnaud.'

She waited for him to go on.

'It's Fred,' Rowan said.

'Fred—what has he done?'

David released a low whistle. 'He's—there's no other way to say it—he's been murdered.'

The blood drained from her face.

'Are you certain?'

'There's no doubt about it,' Oscar said.

She frowned at him.

'This is Oscar Tremont,' David said. 'He's—a consultant working for me.'

'David,' Oscar said, putting a hand on his shoulder. 'I'm going to need to talk to everyone—' He shot a glance at the gendarmes. 'That is, I'm going to need to have an informal chat with everyone in the village in a discreet fashion.'

'I get you,' David said. He turned back to Nina. 'I've hired Oscar Tremont on a personal matter. He's a private detective.'

'This is in connection with Fred's death?' she asked. 'I don't understand. How did you know there was going to be a murder?'

'There's no reason to believe there's a connection at this time,' Oscar said, hoping he sounded convincing.

'Who would want to kill Fred?' she asked.

They shook their heads.

'No one,' Rowan said. 'Honestly.'

'Does Barbara know?' she asked.

The policewoman was knocking at the door while Thérèse watched on, hand over mouth.

No one answered.

'They're going to break the door down if she doesn't answer,' Rowan said. 'You don't suppose—?'

'Don't you dare!' Nina said a little too loudly, and everyone looked their way. 'Don't even think it,' she whispered.

'Does she stay away from home sometimes?' Oscar asked.

'Oh!' Nina chirped. 'You're right. I forgot she told me she was visiting her parents this weekend.' And she hurried over to the policewoman.

'They'll find his headless body in there,' David said, wincing. 'Poor Fred. It's an atrocious end to meet.'

Oscar looked him in the eye. 'You really think so?'

'Of course! It's a horrible way to go!'

'That's not what I mean, David'

'What *do* you mean then? You're always talking in riddles, man!'

'Am I?' Oscar asked, intentionally provoking him.

'Yes!'

'Take it easy, Dad,' Rowan hissed under his breath, seeing that everyone was looking at them. 'Oscar?'

'I mean to ask whether you really think they'll find him in there.'

'I don't know.' David shrugged. 'It's natural to think he was murdered in his home.'

Oscar nodded, satisfied.

'You don't agree, Oscar?' Rowan asked. He was relieved to see that all eyes had turned back to the police cordon.

'I agree that it's a reasonable assumption, but there is little doubt in my mind that he was murdered elsewhere and even less that the gendarmes will eventually find his body elsewhere—unless I beat them to it.'

'Did you find a clue?' Rowan asked.

'I did,' he replied, and his moustache twitched mischievously.

'You told us you didn't take anything but photos,' David reminded him.

'I didn't lie,' Oscar replied, flipping his flat cap off and holding it over his heart. 'I didn't lay a finger on it.'

'You left if for the gendarmes to find in order to put them to the test?'

He grinned. 'That I did, and find it they will.'

'But?' David asked.

'But will they see it for what it is? *Seeing* a clue is not the same as *reading* a clue.'

'What do we do now?' Rowan asked.

'Are you both hungry?'

They shook their heads.

'Me neither. David, you'd better stay here. They'll want to take our statements at some stage. You can call us. Rowan, I'd like you to accompany me on a short drive to Kergaillot, followed by a walk along the path to pay Brieg a visit.'

David and Rowan exchanged blank looks.

10. The Hermit

The gendarme who'd cordoned off the scene stared at the Peugeot
403 as it left the grounds of Ker Greno and turned left, but he made
no move to stop them and Oscar told Rowan not to make eye
contact. The gendarme's wasn't the only attention caught. Nina and
Thérèse observed their departure, as did Hervé Guivarc'h, Bruno
Garcia, and a number of other residents who were peering through
their windows. Those who had left early to go to work—including
Arnaud, Denise, and Kevin—would learn of Fred's death later.

'Right here,' Rowan said.

Oscar took the right and followed the road to La Lande.

'She drives like a beauty.'

'Thank you. The upkeep isn't always cheap, but I treat her well.'
He patted the dashboard. 'And she's worth every penny.'

'Down this way,' Rowan said, pointing.

'Is this Pascal Chotard's farm?' Oscar asked as they passed a
broad field with a large stone cottage on the far side.

'It is. You want to talk to him?'

'I wonder whether he's heard about the murder yet.'

'I don't know. Only if someone called him, I suppose, or he
heard the sirens. He didn't come to Greno though.'

'I didn't see him. We'll see later. A chat with Brieg is the priority.'

'You believe—?'

Oscar tutted. 'Hold your horses, young man. This is about
certainties for the moment. I need more of them. But one certainty
I do have already is that Brieg notices what the rest of you don't.
He's free of the veil held in place by lights, white noise, and thick
walls.'

Rowan didn't press the matter. He indicated the way through

Kergaillot, looking at Youna's house and noting that it looked as though they'd all left for the day.

'Your girlfriend's house?' Oscar asked without taking his eyes off the road as far as Rowan could tell.

'You don't miss much, do you?'

'You didn't hire me to miss anything. However, while we're on the subject, I mustn't neglect to ask you the important question I didn't ask you in front of your father.'

'Are you serious?' Rowan asked, genuinely shocked. 'My father didn't kill his own gardener.'

'Interesting reaction,' Oscar said, eyebrows suddenly raised. 'Shall I park here? The street becomes the path just ahead.'

'Yes. Here's fine.'

'What was I saying? Oh, the lady doth protest, and all that.'

'You weren't asking whether I thought my dad was capable of murdering Fred?'

'No. I wasn't,' Oscar said, pulling onto a narrow shoulder to the side of the street. 'Your father isn't the beheading type, despite his obsession with the "old ways" and all that. In any case, Fred's murderer and the Ankou are one and the same.'

'Is this belief or certainty?'

'*Touché*,' Oscar replied, poking Rowan in the ribs. 'This is a gut feeling for the time being.'

'So, belief?'

'Enough gabbing. It's time to stretch our legs.'

Oscar took his camera from the back seat and got out of the car.

They started along the path.

'Woods on either side,' Oscar summarised. 'The marshland lies beyond the trees to our left.'

'Exactly,' Rowan confirmed. 'You can see where the trees end and the reeds begin.'

'I can. What I can't see, however, are any tracks left by cartwheels. The surface is too hard and more leaves are falling all the time.'

'I told you so.'

'Indeed you did.'

105

'You didn't ask the question,' Rowan reminded him.

'No,' Oscar said, clicking his fingers. 'The most obvious question in the world—I simply wanted to know whether anyone had a reason to want Fred dead. Not specifically your father.'

'And yet, you didn't want to ask me in front of him.'

Oscar stopped walking. Rowan did the same.

'He was relieved to discover the head was Fred's.'

'He was?'

Oscar nodded.

'Why?'

'You really have no idea?'

'No. Tell me.'

'Tell you? I'm afraid you're overestimating me there, Rowan. I don't know—yet. I suspect there was some kind of tension between them. Let me be clear. I'm not saying your father is *happy* Fred's dead, but he definitely failed to conceal his relief. He was very tense last night and less so this morning. Strange, isn't it? You'd think learning—if my gut feeling is right—that the Ankou is no practical joke would make him much more nervous.'

'Yes,' Rowan said. 'I don't know what the connection is—between Fred and the Ankou.'

'It can only be your father, somehow,' Oscar said.

'What you're saying is—?'

'I'm saying he needs to follow my instructions to the letter until I get to the bottom of all this.'

Rowan didn't reply. He understood.

'Getting back to Fred,' Oscar said. 'Any enemies?'

'Not that I know of. Everyone liked him. Well—' he looked ahead along the path.

'Brieg?'

'They had a nasty run-in a while back.'

'Can you be a tad more specific than that?'

'It happened at *Le Chêne*.' Rowan released an involuntary chortle. 'Most differences of opinion do around these parts. Brieg doesn't go there much, but he did on this one day. He was most likely selling

106

or trading this, that, or the other for a drink and cigarettes.'

'Details, Rowan—details. When was this?'

He stared up into the oak branches and reflected.

'A couple of weeks perhaps.'

Oscar hummed.

'It was quite animated. You know how it is when two people have a go at each other and everyone has a bit of a laugh and jeer about it until they realise it's heating up.'

'You're painting the picture well now. What was it about?'

'Fred accused Brieg of having trampled all over a front garden he'd landscaped in Kergaillot. The owner is—*was*—one of his best clients. Better than Dad, I'd say. He'd given Fred *carte blanche* to use his imagination and create a stand-out garden. Fred took a Japanese approach, planting spindle and maples, and adding a fish pond with a miniature pagoda and a rock garden.'

'It caught my attention on the way in,' Oscar said. 'Easily the highlight of the village.'

'Fred was talented. He must have gone back and fixed it up for the owner. I don't actually know him and we don't cross paths much. Anyhow, Fred was rather cruel to Brieg, calling him a waste of space and a loser. It gave us all a shock. He's usually such a nice fellow.'

'No one witnessed Brieg trampling over the garden except Fred?'

Rowan shrugged. 'I'm not even sure Fred did. He might have assumed it was Brieg. He said he recognised his boot prints.'

'This is very interesting. Have there been other complaints about Brieg trespassing or damaging property? You've already told me he hasn't been accused of theft.'

'No and no,' Rowan said. 'Not that I'm aware. It's hardly a motivation to commit murder.'

'You'd be surprised what ridiculous things people get killed over,' Oscar replied. 'That said, Brieg strikes me as being thick-skinned. Not the kind of man who lets what others think about him get to him.'

'That's true.'

'It didn't get physical, this altercation?'

'No. From memory, Brieg told him where to shove it and trudged off muttering about how he should have known not to go to the bar in the first place and about hating crowds.'

'There was a crowd?'

Rowan laughed. 'A group of four or five people constitutes a crowd in Brieg's book. I can't remember who was there. Hervé behind the bar. Kevin and Arnaud, probably. Youna was with me.'

'Let's go and see if Brieg is home. That patch of white through the trees there must be his caravan.'

'It is,' Rowan confirmed.

As they reached the caravan, they heard the sound of chopped wood being stacked coming from the other side.

'Brieg!' Rowan called.

'I'm in my back garden.'

'In his *back garden*,' Oscar whispered to Rowan with a laugh. 'I like him. I hope it doesn't turn out to be him.'

They found Brieg restacking a woodpile. The battered sheet of corrugated metal leaning against an elm was clearly going to be used to cover the firewood.

'Oscar Tremont,' he said, eyeing the new acquaintance warily. He dusted his rough hands off and straightened his beanie.

'You didn't hang around once the sirens of the gendarmerie got a bit too loud,' Oscar mused.

'Nothing to hide. It's just that their presence irks me.'

'They have the same effect on me when I'm trying to crack a case, my friend.'

Brieg smiled, and lowered his guard.

'You're not wanted, are you?' Oscar asked, winking for good measure.

'Me? Hah! No one wants me. Are you here to question me?'

'I have no official authority.'

'No, you don't.'

'I know the gendarmerie though, and they're going to write you up as a person of interest the moment they see you.'

'Is that a threat?'

'Not at all, Brieg. It's just that when they don't find the rest of Fred's body in his house, they'll start looking all around here.'

'How do you know his body isn't in the house?'

'Reassuring,' Oscar said.

'What is?'

'That you asked that question.'

'What—you were thinking I did him in?'

'Well, you weren't the best of friends.'

'I'm not the best of friends with anyone. That doesn't mean I go gallivanting around beheading people.'

'No, it doesn't,' Oscar agreed.

'If I wanted someone dead, I'd do it much more tactfully. You wouldn't even know it was murder. I'd simply break into his cottage, go to the freezer, and slip slices of poisonous toadstool into the frozen mixed vegetables.'

Rowan gasped and Oscar clapped his hands together merrily.

'You would!' Oscar bawled. 'Oh, you would—I'm sure of it. Brilliant! Rowan, don't go crossing this man!'

'I don't intend to,' Rowan said, wide-eyed.

'Now,' Oscar said. 'Can I talk to you in private?'

'What?' Rowan said.

'Go for a walk, lad. This is men's business here,' Brieg teased him.

Oscar did one of his moustache-twitching grins. 'Ten minutes.'

'Fine,' Rowan said a little sulkily and wandered back towards Kergaillot.

'Come inside,' Brieg said.

Simple as it was, the caravan had all the comforts a single man of the woods could need. Heating it would have been easy enough. A log or two per night.

'What I'm going to show you stays between us,' Oscar said.

'You have my word as a gentleman.'

'Thank you.' He turned his camera on and showed him one of the photographs he'd taken at the dolmen.

'That's a grey heron feather,' Brieg said.

'I thought so. Strange finding one near the dolmen, isn't it?'

Brieg nodded. 'I'd say so. They don't venture into the village. Grey herons stick to the marshland.'

Oscar hummed.

'I follow you. You think the murderer accidentally left this behind.'

'It's likely. It was around the side a little, not along the path. Only someone who approached the dolmen from the side could have dropped it.'

'Someone putting a severed head on it.'

'Precisely.'

'This someone would have come from the marshes,' Brieg said.

'But not along the path.'

Brieg frowned. 'How do you mean?'

'I know the murderer didn't come to the dolmen from here. Is there another way?'

'Not without cutting through private property. Otherwise, the road into the village is the only way.'

'Nevertheless, you've confirmed what I thought. Grey herons don't stray far from the water.'

Brieg stroked his goatee. 'You think Fred's body is in the marshes?'

'It seems likely. You know the marshes well, I take it?'

'No one knows them better.'

'If a body was weighed down—?'

'You'd never find it,' Brieg said. 'Police divers perhaps.' He shook his head.

'That's what I was afraid you'd say. I'm guessing the head was carried in a bag of some kind and the feather happened to be inside.'

'If Fred was murdered in the marshes, there must be traces of blood along the ground nearby.'

'Unless it happened in the water, which seems unlikely,' Oscar said. 'Was he in the habit of visiting the marshes?'

'Not at all.'

'Interesting. Very interesting.'

'Meeting someone?'

'I'm betting on it.'

'If I see anything, I'll tell you—not the gendarmes.'

'Good man! Now, before Rowan comes back, I have a couple of questions to ask you about the Trevelyan family.'

'Oh,' Brieg said. 'In that case, it's my turn to say this needs to stay between the two of us.'

'Gentleman's oath,' Oscar said, flat cap over heart. 'So, Brieg, how well do you know David and Rowan?'

'As well as one can know folks who've never once invited one in for a drink, let alone dinner—but hey, I'm hardly civilised company. Rowan's all right for a rich kid. What do I know about him? Well, he walks through the woods all the time to visit his sweetheart in Kergaillot. He always stops to give me the time of day, which is more than I can say for some. David's a different story.'

'That's the impression I have. I don't mind telling you it was Rowan's idea to call me about this Ankou business.'

'I'd guessed as much.'

'He suggested you believe in the—some of the old stories.'

'Rowan said that?' Brieg laughed. 'I like to pull his leg—that's all. I'm not as daft as folks think.'

'I know,' Oscar replied, tapping his nose.

'I'm open-minded though. Who are we to pretend to have fathomed the depths of the universe?'

'Quite.'

'But any fanciful notion of the Ankou vanished from my mind this morning.'

'Because the severed head on the dolmen has no foundation in legend,' Oscar pointed out.

'Not a bit,' Brieg confirmed. 'What you're trying to work out is why Fred was killed if your client is the target.'

'That, and why David *is* the target—and whose?'

'He strikes me as a slippery fish. I wouldn't be surprised if he's done wrong by someone.'

111

'Someone in the village?'

Brieg shrugged. 'It's just a vague notion. Someone dressed up as the Ankou to haunt him. That's what happened, isn't it?'

'Apparently so.'

'That's payback. That's wanting him to fear for his life.'

'On the face of it,' Oscar agreed. 'But it's Fred's head I found on the dolmen. You're quite certain he doesn't go for walks through the woods or along the edge of the marshland?'

'I never saw him do that, but that doesn't mean he never did.'

All the same, Oscar was confident Brieg would have noticed if he was doing that on a regular basis. Unless he was doing it secretly and was meeting up with someone—the same someone who killed him. And killed him why? Because he got in the way? He didn't want to go through with it?

Footsteps sounded on the path.

'That's Rowan,' Oscar said.

Brieg nodded. 'You have a good ear.'

They left the caravan.

'Ten minutes already?' Oscar asked.

'More or less,' said Rowan.

'Thank you for your time and candour, Brieg.' Oscar touched the brim of his cap.

'I'll let you know if I learn anything, but while the crime scene is cordoned off, I'm stuck here.'

'They won't leave the path blocked for long. Be careful, Brieg.'

'I'll be fine. You're the ones who need to watch your step.'

'Truer words. We'll let you get back to stacking your wood.'

As they returned to the path, Oscar thought about what he'd just said. It reminded him of a lead he had to chase up.

11. The Gendarmerie

As they walked back to Kergaillot, Oscar wondered how much progress the gendarmerie had made. The investigative team must have arrived and started taking statements. The forensics squad would be scouring the area. Would Fred's wife have been informed by now?

'They didn't have children?'

'Fred and Barbara? No. I think they'd been trying. She'll know by now, I guess.'

'I was just thinking about that.'

'Dad hasn't called.'

'I get the feeling the gendarmerie is happy to keep me out of the picture. That could change as the investigation proceeds. Time will tell. Finding the body and murder weapon will be the priority.'

Oscar stopped and surveyed a stretch of the marshland that could be seen through a gap in the trees. Tall grass and saplings grew in the clearing, and where it met the path, there was a thick layer of leaves.

'That's odd,' he said.

'What is?'

'This opening here.'

'Access to the marsh. That's all.'

'I don't have an issue with that, but walking back this way, I've noticed something that escaped me coming from Kergaillot. Don't you see what I mean?'

Rowan looked carefully. The clearing was wide enough for a tractor to turn around. The grass was tall and oak saplings grew here and there. There was green tarpaulin stretched out across a pile of gravel. Where the path dipped at the edge—not as deep as the ditch but a dip all the same—the fallen leaves were thick.

'The leaves?' he asked.

Oscar raised his eyebrows. 'What about them?'

'There are more along the edge here than before and after the clearing, even though there are no trees at this particular spot.'

Oscar gave him a pat on the back. 'Now, that really is quite odd, don't you think?'

'A little,' he admitted. 'It could be the wind.'

Oscar didn't reply. He walked over to the edge of the path and started clearing the leaves away with his hands. A narrow impression to the right was soon exposed.

'No!' Rowan said.

Oscar cleared the leaves away a few feet to the left and found an identical mark. He stood up, brushed his hands off, and looked at Rowan. 'Cartwheel tracks.'

'But where did it go?'

'Let's have a look.'

Oscar waded gently through the tall grass, trying to see where it had been squashed, but he couldn't make out any clear tracks. A tractor had passed recently. That was easy to see by the broad ruts and tyre marks. There were also a number of hoof prints, and judging by the varying sizes, they belonged to more than one horse. Deciphering the landscape wouldn't be possible. The best Oscar could hope for was to catch sight of the cartwheel tracks further along.

'It can't have vanished into thin air,' Rowan said.

'No,' Oscar replied. 'That, it can't have done. Check the pile of gravel, please.'

Rowan tapped his hand against the tarpaulin. It felt rough and solid. There was gravel all around the base, spilling out from under the tarpaulin.

Oscar turned to the marshland. There was a grey heron stalking through the water—ready to snap up prey with its long beak.

'The cart may have been manoeuvred here and then continued along the path,' Rowan suggested.

114

'But why?' Oscar asked.

Rowan shrugged.

The sound of voices and footsteps distracted Oscar from his contemplation, and two gendarmes came into view a moment later. One was short and had a sniffer dog on a leash. The other was tall and wore a scowl that Oscar suspected may have been permanent. He couldn't hear exactly what they were saying, but he thought he caught the words "suspicious" and "bum".

'Hello there,' the tall one said as they arrived at the clearing. 'Gendarmerie Nationale,' he added superfluously.

'Good morning,' Oscar replied. These weren't the two male policeman who had arrived with Major Faure.

'Have you lost something?' the one with the dog asked.

'No,' Oscar answered quickly. 'We're just out for a stroll—clearing our heads.'

'You know there's a murder investigation under way?'

'I'm the one who found the head,' Oscar said. 'That's why we're here, keeping out of your hair.'

The tall gendarme whispered to the one with the dog, who in turn looked at Oscar and frowned.

There was no point pretending otherwise. 'My name is Oscar Tremont.'

'We thought so,' the tall gendarme said.

'I'm flattered.'

'No.' The permanent scowl intensified. 'I didn't recognise you. We were briefed about you.'

'Major Faure?'

'Correct.'

'I don't get the impression he's a fan of my work.'

The gendarmes came closer and noticed the cartwheel tracks. That didn't seem to interest them, however. Why would it? They were looking for Fred's body. It confirmed Oscar's suspicion that no one would mention hearing the horse and cart the previous two nights. What caught Oscar's attention most of all was the dog's behaviour—it was sitting calmly at its handler's feet.

'I'm not interfering with your investigation.'

'That's what we wanted to hear, sir.'

'Fine animal,' Oscar said.

'She is,' the handler said. 'She's very clever. I'd venture to say the best detective in the world.'

Oscar smiled. And yet, she wasn't reacting to any scent.

'You're looking for the rest of his body?'

'We can't comment on—'

'Of course not,' Oscar interrupted. 'I didn't mean to be rude. Nevertheless, if we find it, we'll leave the scene uncontaminated and inform you immediately '

'We understand each other then.'

With that, they continued along the path.

'Did you notice?' Rowan asked once they were out of earshot.

'I certainly did,' Oscar said with a grin. 'And I'm glad you did too.'

'This means Fred's body isn't here.'

'That's right, and it means he wasn't decapitated here. Unless—' Oscar peered out across the water.

'Unless it happened in the marshes and there's no longer any trace of blood or Fred's odour.'

Oscar nodded. 'It's a long shot. It doesn't, however, mean the horse and cart didn't come this way.'

'No,' Rowan admitted. 'Where does this leave us?'

'It leaves us where we were already.' Oscar walked to the water's edge—or rather, to where the ground was so damp his cherry red Doc Martens began to sink in.

'You're wondering whether it could have been transported on a barge, aren't you?' Rowan asked.

'I'm not the only one with a vivid imagination,' Oscar replied.

He walked around the clearing, but there was nowhere a cart could have been stowed away. There was no gap wide enough for a cart to pass through in the frontline of trees and bushes separating clearing from woods and reaching from path to marsh. Drawing a deep breath, he turned from the elms and oaks, holly and gorse, and

116

retreated to the tracks at the path's edge.

'I think you're right, Rowan. The cart was manoeuvred here.'

They stared at the two impressions, trying to visualise what had happened.

'Are there any abandoned houses in Kergaillot?' Oscar asked.

'I don't think so.'

Oscar walked to the middle of the path and looked up and down its length as far as he could see. Hiding the cart closer to Brieg's caravan would be foolish. He started walking back to Kergaillot. There were trees on both sides of the path as well as an unbroken ditch.

'Where to now?' Rowan asked once they reached the car.

The gendarmes were walking back through the village now.

'The trail grows cold,' Oscar mused.

'We could see if Pascal Chotard is at home. I don't know him well though.'

'It could be useful to get his opinion on the impressions. He's the only person who'd be able to assert beyond the shadow of a doubt that they were caused by his cart merely by measuring their width and distance apart.'

He turned the key in the ignition and did a three-point turn. As he passed the gendarmes, he gave them a friendly wave which wasn't returned.

'I thought we'd reached an understanding,' Oscar remarked. 'I don't think they like me.'

'I'm not sure you really convinced them,' Rowan pointed out. 'Regardless, they're gendarmes—they don't like anyone.'

'Fair point. Ah, look who's out riding while the world burns around her.'

'You know Jessica?'

'Only from your description—an elegant raven-haired girl on a mare of midnight black.'

'I said that?'

'Something along those lines. I'm prone to a touch of poetic licence every once in a while.'

'I get the feeling you do that quite a lot.'

'Only with details that don't require precision, of course. It depends on the situation. It's the vibe of the thing, your Honour!'

'What?'

Oscar shook his head. 'You haven't been watching your Australian cinematic classics. Tut-bloody-tut! What's more—the line is uttered by a fine solicitor.'

'I'll look it up,' Rowan said unenthusiastically.

Oscar pulled up on the side of the street and got out of the car in order to wait for Jessica and engage her in conversation without spooking Minuit. Rowan followed him.

'Hello,' Jessica said as she drew closer. Oscar thought there was a hint of suspicion in her voice, but she visibly relaxed on recognising Rowan.

'Good morning, mademoiselle. She's a beauty.'

Jessica stroked Minuit's mane.

'My name is Oscar Tremont. You know Rowan, of course. I'm a private investigator working for the Trevelyans. I was wondering whether you couldn't spare a couple of minutes.'

She looked from Oscar to Rowan and back again. 'It's about Fred Gaillo?'

'It's about your father's stolen cart. But if you have any information about Fred's death?'

She shook her head. 'You've found the cart?'

'We've found what appear to be cartwheel tracks down by the marshland, on the edge of the path.'

'How strange!'

'Why do you say that?'

'Well, I wouldn't have expected the thief to take the cart by hand and head down to the marsh. Dad assumed it was a professional burglary and that the cart had been loaded onto a lorry and carried away.'

Oscar nodded. It was the most logical assumption to make after all.

'I don't understand,' she said. 'What are you investigating?'

118

Rowan and Oscar exchanged a look and came to an unspoken agreement.

'On two occasions, someone dressed as the Ankou stopped outside my father's bedroom window and waved a scythe at him.'

'Are you serious?'

'Dead serious. You know what the Ankou is supposed to look like according to legend?'

'Death,' Jessica hissed, and Oscar was sure she remembered her brother at that moment. 'Death riding a cart!'

'Exactly,' Oscar said, studying her face. 'You see?'

'Yes,' she answered, seeming to shiver.

'A cart drawn by a black horse,' he added.

She stroked Minuit's mane again and Oscar noticed a frown form under the brim of her riding hat.

'A completely black horse,' Rowan hastened to say. 'Not like Minuit with a white streak.'

She didn't reply.

'Is your father available?' Oscar asked.

'He's not home at the moment.'

'I'd like him to identify the tracks. He might be able to confirm his cart made them.'

'It's where the path is nearest the marshland?'

'Yes. There's a clearing.'

'I know where you mean. I'll tell him.'

'Thank you,' Oscar said, touching the brim of his flat cap. 'Oh, and I'll have a question or two to ask you about horse grooming, but that can wait for another time.'

'No problem,' she said. 'Ah, do you have a horse?'

'No. My interest is purely professional.'

'Okay. When you're ready.'

'As for Fred Gaillo—any idea who wanted him dead?' Oscar sprang the question without warning.

'None,' she answered immediately.

'You've already thought about it?'

'Naturally. I mean, when someone's head turns up on a dolmen

119

overnight, you can't help but wonder who put it there.'

'No, you can't,' Oscar agreed. 'It makes you think back to past conflicts, one of which—with the benefit of hindsight—you realise may have been the trigger.'

'I didn't know Fred well. He did some work around the farm for us on rare occasions, like a lot of the men in the area. There were never any issues. Whoever killed him must be the same person riding around dressed as the Ankou,' she said. 'Right?'

'It seems likely.'

She looked at Rowan. 'This means—'

'Yes,' Oscar said gravely. 'Rowan's father is taking every precaution.'

'Am I in danger, Monsieur Tremont?'

'I can't see why you would be, but I'd suggest staying indoors after dark for the time being.'

'I generally do, but that's not very reassuring.'

'It isn't,' Oscar admitted.

'This is some kind of psychopath. It has to be,' Jessica said.

'Why do you say that?' Rowan asked.

'Riding around dressed up as the Ankou. Threatening your father but killing Fred. There's no sense to it.'

'Mark my words, Jessica—there is method here, and there is motivation,' Oscar told her. 'It may appear there's neither rhyme nor reason to what's happening, but I'll eventually find a pattern and catch our killer. Whether or not it makes sense to us is another question, but the reason for Fred's death and the threats levelled at David Trevelyan will come to light. However strange this all is, there's nothing random about it. As for being a psychopath—' Oscar paused. 'Ultimately, the mental state of the accused is up to a court of justice to decide.'

Rowan sighed. 'First, we have to catch him.'

'That's the most pressing matter,' Oscar said. 'Thank you for your time, Jessica. Please let me know once your father has had a look at the tracks.'

'I will. Good luck.'

'Thank you. A little luck always helps.'

They watched Jessica and Minuit continue along the street. The gentle clopping of hooves marked a steady beat.

'What do you think?' Rowan asked.

Oscar tapped his nose. 'All in good time, young man. All in good time. I'd rather dazzle you with facts than hunches.'

Rowan's gaze was fixed on the rider and her mare, but Oscar could tell by his expression that his thoughts were focused on interpreting the meaning of that last sentence.

'We didn't learn a thing just now,' Rowan said after a moment, but his uncertainty was palpable.

'Didn't we?' Oscar mused. 'Learn—it's an interesting word.'

'I wish you'd stop doing that.'

'You mean being cryptic?'

'Yes! At least you realise you're doing it.'

'I'm a married man. I don't need to do meditation or yoga to have my failings revealed to me.'

'That's a story I know.'

'We don't choose our fathers, Rowan. We do what we can with the one we have, and while we have him.'

Rowan gave him a quizzical look.

'This is a chat we might have one day, and I promise I won't be too cryptic. But I can't tell you what I don't know, and some mysteries are harder to solve than others.'

'Perhaps this will be one of them.'

'It won't be,' Oscar said confidently.

'How do you know that?'

'Gut feeling.'

'Gut feeling?'

Oscar nodded. 'Not everything can be neatly measured and labelled. Sometimes, you just have to follow your nose. While Jessica didn't give us any concrete information, she did get me thinking. Like I said, I want to see where it leads—if it leads anywhere at all.' Oscar looked up and down the street. 'Talking about following noses, I wonder if that dog has found the rest of

Fred yet.'

'I was counting on you to beat her to it,' Rowan teased.

'Finding Fred's remains isn't my priority. Solving his murder is.'

Rowan thought about that. 'The answer doesn't necessary lie where Fred does.'

'I looked out the bedroom window and saw his head on display for your father. You know what the severed head represented for the ancient Celts, and most Iron Age cultures?'

'The head was venerated as the seat of the soul, and when a warrior vanquished an enemy, he commonly hung the severed head around his horse's neck as a trophy.'

Oscar hummed. 'Precisely. They were also kept in chests or proudly displayed inside homes. Was Fred's head placed on the dolmen as a victorious boast?'

Rowan took his time before answering.

'I wouldn't say so,' he said. 'It was intended as an outrage. No—that's not quite it. It was a warning.'

'That's right. Why Fred was killed is yet to be established, but the reason his head was put on the dolmen was to terrify your father—and that is not strictly in keeping with tradition.'

'What you're saying is that whoever is impersonating the Ankou isn't as thoroughly versed in Celtic lore as my father?'

'Or you, or me, or Brieg. In fact, Brieg made it very clear that it was the apparition of Fred's head on the dolmen that convinced him it couldn't really be the Ankou at large. It's someone putting on a hell of a show and going to great lengths to curse your father with his own obsession, but not quite getting it right.'

'Does that get us anywhere?' Rowan asked.

'It's worth keeping in mind. Our killer is someone who has an incomplete understanding of lore.'

'And who is using it as a conduit for exacting revenge on my dad.'

Oscar thought again about how David's attitude had changed that morning when he saw that it was Fred's head on the dolmen—relief and bewilderment.

'Are we ready to head back to Ker Greno?' Rowan asked.
'I think we are. My appetite has returned.'
'So has mine,' Rowan said. 'Life must go on.'
'That's the spirit. Keep calm and carry on.'

12. Tea with Princess Diana

One of Oscar's questions was answered before his Peugeot 403 had even entered the grounds of Ker Greno. He parked by the salt cedar, no longer needing to hide his presence.

'Your father will be in the library.'

'No doubt about it. You want me to check on him while you ask the gendarmes where the body was found?'

Oscar shook his head. 'I'd rather ask your old man. It can't hurt for you to stick your nose about out there though.'

They got out of the car.

'Not so hungry after all?' Rowan asked.

'A light lunch will do. Sandwiches or the like. But I won't be able to eat until I know.'

Oscar tried to open the door to the house but found it locked. He called to Rowan, who was already walking along the drive. 'You got the key?'

'It's locked? That's not like Dad to lock up in the middle of the day.'

'He's either playing it very safe or he's letting the police know he doesn't want to be disturbed.'

Rowan came back to unlock the door but David arrived downstairs at the same moment and opened up.

'How are you holding up?' Oscar asked.

'I'm burying myself in my work.' The ensuing grimace told Oscar he'd immediately regretted employing that particular verb. 'Come on in. Do you have any news?'

'I do have some, but you first.'

'You haven't heard?'

'No,' Oscar replied, immediately grasping his meaning. 'When did they find it?'

'A quarter of an hour ago or thereabouts, floating in the marsh just behind Brieg's caravan.'

Oscar thought it peculiar that the greatest—if not humblest—detective in the world hadn't sniffed it out the first time round. But as they say, perfection is not of this world.

'I've never trusted him—'

'But you know it's not him.'

David didn't reply.

'Who told you?'

'Thérèse. She wouldn't divulge her source.'

'It must be the young policewoman.'

'That's my guess.'

'We can rely on it as true then.'

Oscar remembered his laser alarm. If Fred had been murdered in or near the marsh, as both the heron feather and the location of his corpse indicated, the killer had then taken the long way around and into the village before placing his skull on the dolmen—or he'd cut through gardens.

'There you go,' Oscar said distractedly.

'Where to from here?' David asked.

'A light lunch is in order if you don't mind.'

'I've already eaten, but Rowan will look after you.'

'He's a fine young man.'

David nodded. 'He is. He really is. He'll be all right.'

Oscar wasn't quite sure what David meant by that last part but decided not to react.

'Did Thérèse mention Fred's wife?'

'She was with her parents after all. I expect the gendarmes have called on her.'

'Poor woman. I expect we won't see her back in the village today.'

'I imagine she'll stay with her folks a while.'

'Your news?'

Oscar told him as much as he wanted him to know.

125

'Give me your professional opinion. What are the chances the gendarmerie will catch him?'

'It's a tough call. Being a branch of the armed forces, the gendarmerie specialises in performing routine controls and tracking down fugitives in rural environments. Their success in a murder investigation generally depends on the work of their forensics team. The problem they face here is the nature of the affair. We're not talking about your typical criminal, are we? They've managed to find the rest of Fred's body without too much difficulty, but that may not give them much to go on. If they combed the countryside, I don't doubt they would find the horse and cart, and possibly the murder weapon.'

'It's out of the question, Oscar,' David said calmly but severely. 'I won't be made a laughing stock.'

'You do appreciate that by holding our tongues, we're obstructing the course of justice?'

'I understand,' he replied drily. 'It's not too late for you to walk away, Oscar.'

'It is,' Oscar said. 'It most definitely is too late. But even if it weren't, I wouldn't consider it for a second. I'll solve this mystery. I only hope I can do so without any further bloodshed.'

David looked to the floor in silence, then lifted his gaze to meet Oscar's. 'You do what you can. My plan is to keep my head down and make progress on my book.'

'I'm glad to hear that,' Oscar replied.

The sound of the door being opened and closed reached their ears from downstairs.

'Is that you, Rowan?' David called.

Oscar noted the nervous edge to his voice.

'Yes. It's just me, Dad. Are you coming down for lunch?'

'Already eaten. You look after Oscar.'

'Are you working?'

'Sitting around twiddling my thumbs isn't going to bring Fred back.'

'No,' Rowan said after a moment, barely loud enough to be heard in the library. 'Leave him to it, Oscar!' he called out.

'May the muse be with you,' Oscar said.

'*Awen*, if you don't mind.'

'*Ya. Gwir eo*,' Oscar replied, and he held his right hand up with three fingers pointing downwards to represent rays of light.

David nodded approvingly. 'Are those three scars on the back of your right hand a manifestation of Awen?'

Oscar remained stone-faced. 'No more than the scar on the back of your head where no hair grows.'

The blood drained from David's face.

'We all have our secrets,' Oscar told him with a wicked wink. He then smiled charmingly. 'I'll bring you a cup of tea later.'

Oscar took his leave and went downstairs to join Rowan, reminding himself that while inspiration always proved helpful in elucidating a mystery, insight was crucial.

'Did the gendarmes feel like sharing?'

'Not especially,' Rowan answered. 'Ham and cheese toasty? It's beechwood smoked ham.'

'Perfect. Thanks.'

'They know that whatever they tell me will be leaked straight to you.'

'It's such a shame.'

'How do you mean?'

'Do you know why I became a private investigator, Rowan?'

He thought about it while he spread salted butter on a slice of bread. 'I guess because you've always enjoyed solving puzzles?'

Oscar clicked his fingers, almost making Rowan jump. 'Spot on! Now, I'm not saying none of them got into the game for the same reason, but the red tape and routine must have smothered the flames of those who had one to begin with.'

'Luckily for us, there's someone in town whose flame hasn't been smothered,' Rowan said with a laugh.

'Thérèse Derrien,' Oscar said. 'Your father told me.'

'Cheddar or Emmental?'

'Cheddar, please.'

'I was thinking about calling my mother and catching up on my studies this afternoon,' Rowan said apologetically.

'Of course. You need to take your mind off all this, and you mustn't fall behind with your coursework. I'll keep myself busy. I have a line of enquiry to follow.'

Rowan put the sandwiches into the sandwich toaster and Oscar decided to cast a line. He looked at the back of his right hand.

'I noticed that,' Rowan said when he turned back from the toaster. 'Nasty scratches.'

Oscar nodded. 'Not my fondest memory,' he said. 'You don't have any scars yet?'

'Fingers crossed,' Rowan said. 'None yet. Dad has one on the back of his head. No doubt you've noticed.'

'Now that you mention it, I did notice,' Oscar said. 'Do you know how it happened?'

Rowan shrugged. 'He says he doesn't remember.'

'Oh. It mustn't have been too dramatic then. Those smell great.'

'Nothing like a toasty for a quick lunch. I've got a couple of bottles of beer in the fridge if you're interested.'

'I won't say no to that.'

Rowan made a point of avoiding any talk of the investigation while they ate for both their sakes.

'I'll leave you to it, Rowan,' Oscar said once they'd finished. 'Oh, I almost forgot—I told your father I'd take a cup of tea up to him after lunch.'

'I'll do it. You want one?'

'Maybe later.'

'Suit yourself.'

'I need to pop back home later,' Oscar said. 'I won't be long though. I think I'd best stay here again tonight.'

'You think he'll come back so soon after—'

'I think it's likely, unless the forensics team hasn't finished with the scene.'

'They won't stay in the village all night?'

'That's not how it works. Their job is to gather evidence and analyse it. The gendarmerie won't esteem that the village is at risk and in need of around-the-clock surveillance. You wouldn't believe how much it costs per hour to keep a unit mobilised.'

'I'll be here to let you in,' Rowan said.

Oscar frowned. 'Your father will be as well, won't he?'

'I don't know—oh, of course, I'll—'

'He's not to wander off anywhere without you,' Oscar said. 'Is that clear?'

'Crystal.'

'Good.'

And with that, Oscar took his flat cap and jacket. He left the house and walked slowly to his car. Once inside, he started it up and sat there peering from the kitchen window to the library window and back again. Confident that neither Rowan nor David was watching, he put the car into gear and drove around to the far side of the garage, where he cut the engine.

Parked hugging the garage, the Peugeot couldn't be seen from any window in the house. The object of his interest, however, could be. What remained of the dovecote stood several feet to the right. If either of the Trevelyan men caught him poking around in there, he could simply claim he was inspecting the grounds and that he'd moved his car because he was worried the birds that frequented the salt cedar might go on a bombing raid. After all, that wasn't untrue.

The objective, however, was to work out why David had been so obviously trying to keep Oscar's attention from the ruined building, and to do it in secret. More than once since he'd arrived, David's body language and near slips of the tongue had indicated that the dovecote was a source of distress.

He took a torch from the glove compartment, got out of the car, and checked that David wasn't sipping his tea at the window. Seeing that the coast was clear, he strode over to the dovecote and switched the torch on as he ducked under the blue tarpaulin.

Wood was stacked on pallets arranged in a horseshoe shape so that only the entrance to the dovecote and the middle of the round floor was clear. It was to the floor that Oscar pointed his torch. It was covered in woodchip and pine bark. In the dead centre was a chopping block. The wood was stacked neatly on the pallets and only the stack immediately to the right of the entrance was a little shorter than the others. The pallet to the left of the door only held a half stack, and on that pallet was a deep wicker basket full of dried branches and thin splinters for kindling. An axe was leaning against the basket.

'You were a neat chap, dear Fred,' Oscar muttered under his breath. 'You paid attention to detail. Was that what caused your downfall? Did you see something you shouldn't have?'

He swept every inch of the wood stacks with his torch, looking for the detail he needed. The roosting niches would be the obvious place to conceal a small object, but that was just it—too obvious. If it was Fred who was stacking the wood, he'd notice anything nestled in one of the niches for the simple reason that all the others were empty.

Oscar found himself pointing the torch at the cutting block. He stared at it as though hypnotised by the criss-cross of axe marks on the surface. After several seconds, he put the torch on the floor and wrestled the cutting block to one side, then used his foot to scrape at the hardened earth. It was solid, but it didn't ring true. It didn't feel right. He grabbed the axe and dug at the ground with its head, and he immediately understood. There was a plank of wood.

'Here we go,' he said, using the axe to scratch the earth away and expose the contours of the plank.

He pulled one end up and pivoted the plank until he could rest the end against the cutting block. He then took the torch and looked into the small hole, no bigger than a shoebox. There was a small piece of tarpaulin the same blue as the one covering the dovecote. He gently lifted it to expose a tea tin with a battered portrait of Princess Diana on each of the four sides.

Oscar prised it open and shone the torch into it. There was a tiny square of folded paper. He removed it and unfolded it ever so carefully.

'It is as I suspected,' he whispered to himself, and he couldn't

130

help but feel a pang of remorse.

He was still examining his find when he heard the unmistakable sound of gravel being crunched under the sole of a shoe—and it had come from nearby.

He had his back to the entrance, so couldn't see outside, but without moving, he turned his attention from the paper to the ground. There had been a slight shift in the gentle daylight coming through the opening. It was almost imperceptible from his position, but the noise he'd heard confirmed it wasn't a figment of his imagination. A faint shadow had been cast over the woodchip and pine bark, producing much the same effect as a wisp of cloud passing between the winter sun and the leaf litter of a forest floor.

He let the paper slip from his fingers, and when he spun around, he saw the legs of a pair of blue jeans and a pair of worn-out black work boots. It wasn't Rowan or David, and it definitely wasn't a gendarme.

He steeled himself to spring into action, disappointed that the identity of the culprit in what had become one of the most singular cases of his career was to be revealed to him in such an uncouth fashion.

But he accepted that this was how it was to be.

He snatched up the axe and charged at the legs, but one of the boots kicked out and caught him on the forehead, sending him crashing back to the floor of the dovecote. The only slight consolation was that the instant before it made contact, the heel of the boot caught the brim of his flat cap and pulled it down over his face, lessening the force of the impact.

Oscar had managed to keep a hold of the axe and he held it up horizontally with outstretched arms, ready to defend himself as best he could despite being flat on his back.

But when he raised his head and looked at the entrance, he saw unobstructed daylight. He winced and touched his head—above all to make sure it was still there—and then he struggled to his feet and rushed out.

It was too late. His assailant was nowhere to be seen.

131

All he knew was that he hadn't fled along the drive. There hadn't been enough time to escape that way unseen, and it would have aroused suspicion, fleeing the grounds of Ker Greno through the village with the police all over the place and the likes of Thérèse Derrien keeping watch.

Where then?

Oscar hurried around the dovecote and scanned the woodland area behind the Trevelyan grounds. It was the only other way. But it was too late. There was no one to be seen. This was someone who knew the lay of the land like the back of his hand and was brazen enough to attack in broad daylight.

He felt his forehead and went back into the dovecote to check the state of his flat cap, wondering whether without it he would now be in possession of a clear sample of the boot print stamped on his forehead. He brushed the dirt and flecks of bark off his cap and put it back on.

Looking on the bright side, his head was still attached to his body and he'd succeeded in ruffling feathers. Fred's killer clearly felt threatened by his presence and knew he wasn't in the dovecote to collect firewood. It had been a warning, and Oscar was in no doubt that if there were to be another encounter, it wouldn't be a mere boot he'd have to reckon with.

He folded the piece of paper, put it back in the tea tin, and did his best to make it look like he'd never discovered it at all. Once the cutting block was back in place and the woodchip and bark smoothed out around it, he cautiously left the dovecote.

A glance at the library window sufficed to confirm that David hadn't witnessed the incident. Oscar traced the route his assailant had taken off the grounds as best he could. There was always the slim chance he'd stepped in a patch of mud and left a nice boot print or dropped an item by accident.

He kept his torch gripped in his right hand. His attacker was almost certainly long gone by now, weaving his way through some narrow marshland track, but his sore head reminded him not to take any risks.

It didn't take long for him to realise there was nothing to be found. In any case, he appreciated that he was up against a clever opponent who was unlikely to make too many foolish mistakes. The grey heron feather was likely a one-off, if it hadn't been planted as a red herring. After making Oscar so intimately acquainted with his work boots, he wouldn't be in hurry to wear them again. All the same, Oscar made a mental note to observe everyone's footwear even more attentively from now on.

He followed the hedge along to the corner of the property and found a gap allowing him to glimpse the path and dolmen. The gendarme standing guard yawned, and on the other side of the police tape, the forensics team was starting to pack up. As he'd expected, they wouldn't be staying in the village much longer.

There was a lot to get done before nightfall, and judging by the killer's brazenness, Oscar no longer entertained the faintest shadow of a doubt that the Ankou would ride again that night.

13. Vanishing Act

Oscar checked his forehead in the left-hand wing mirror of his car. It was a little red, but he was confident it wouldn't be noticeable as long as he was wearing his flat cap. Even if someone asked him about it, he could easily claim he'd lost his footing while walking along the edge of the marshes and hit his head on the trunk of a tree. All the same, he preferred to be the one asking the questions.

He slipped his torch into the kangaroo pocket of his jacket and wandered casually along the drive and out onto the street. He stopped by the village oven and was surprised to discover the gendarmes no longer had an audience. When he glanced at Thérèse Derrien's cottage, there was no indication that she was home at all. It was the same story for her neighbours—the Guivarc'hs, the Moisons, and Kevin Barazer.

Oscar pulled his phone out and held it up, pretending to be checking for a signal while actually watching the forensics team pack up. If either Fred's head or the rest of his body held any secrets, they would be discovered in the lab. For his part, Oscar had two immediate goals—to ascertain the identity of the Ankou and to gather evidence during and after its next imminent outing. His challenge was to accomplish both of these goals without putting himself or anyone else in harm's way.

A yellow postal van arrived in the village and the postwoman slowed down and stared at the crime scene before delivering a letter to the Moisons. She then performed a tight three-point turn and drove back out of the village.

Oscar watched the van disappear from view and kept his gaze fixed on the street as though trying to read some deeper meaning into the ordinary occurrence. In his mind, he replayed the conversations he'd had that day. He revisited Brieg in his caravan and stood looking up at Jessica straddling Minuit. He went up to the library and checked on David. Then there was the conversation he hadn't had—the kick in the face—which boiled down to being the most open and honest exchange of them all.

He recalled the horror that had been exhibited to him that dawn, and he saw the look of bewilderment and relief on David's face.

There were already enough pieces to the puzzle for him to take a stab at what the picture looked like.

He slipped his phone back into his jacket pocket and leaned back against the bread oven, his hands clasped together. He continued exploring the pieces in his mind, trying to fit them together, and he pushed his palms together as he did so, as though arm-wrestling himself. His left hand advanced, but his right hand ended up countering and his attention was drawn to the three slick scars on the back of it.

A frown formed on his brow and he let his arms drop to his sides. He was contemplating one particular piece that slotted into another.

He pushed himself away from the bread oven and turned to ponder the line-up of cottages. He stroked his moustache. There were secrets within these quaint country homes—past the garden gates and up the paved paths, under those thatched roofs and behind the blue, green, or burgundy doors. They all held tea tins of their own.

Oscar's task was to work out which home contained a secret that fit in with this affair, and the more he thought about it, the more it all started to come together.

#

He returned to Ker Greno shortly before sunset. He used his phone to take a photo of his forehead and check how it looked before he knocked on the door—as good as brand spanking new, as far as he was concerned.

'Where did you disappear to for so long?' Rowan asked when he

135

opened the door. 'Did you go home?'

'It wasn't necessary after all,' he replied. 'My priority is to get to the bottom of this case and make sure I don't let my boys down by missing out on Halloween. No—I've been for a walk.'

'How far did you go?'

'Far enough to straighten out my head and hatch a plan. The Ankou will ride tonight, Rowan—make no mistake about it—and we won't be taken by surprise this time.'

'You want to confront him?' Rowan asked wide-eyed.

Oscar shook his head. 'That would be too risky, and I don't only mean for me—let's not forget that the horse is an innocent party in all this.'

'That's true.'

'By the same token, we mustn't underestimate its role,' Oscar said.

He put his jacket and flat cap on the coat rack and let Rowan mull over what he'd said.

'We're still talking about the horse?'

'Well, *I* am,' Oscar replied.

'What do you need me to do?' Rowan asked. 'Herbal tea?'

'Yes, please. Your father's upstairs?'

Rowan nodded.

'Good.' Oscar sat at the table. 'You're good on a bike, aren't you?'

'Not bad, I suppose. You want me to follow the Ankou?'

'Preferably without being seen.'

Rowan put the kettle on.

'You're not to try to catch up with him. The aim is to get a rough idea where the cart leaves the track.'

'I get the distinct impression not being able to fathom that little problem is what bothers you the most.'

Oscar smiled wanly. 'I don't like being outsmarted.'

'What are you going to do?'

'I'm going to occupy your father's room again.'

'You want to know exactly what he saw?' Rowan asked quietly.

'Correct. I need to feel threatened the way he did.'

136

'If we pull it off—the Ankou believes you're my dad, and I manage to follow him until he leaves the track—but what happens next? We wait until daylight to try to uncover the cart?'

'You return to Ker Greno and tell me what you saw, and then you stay put here with your father until morning. If you're spotted—which I doubt you will be—you get off the track as quickly as possible, even if it means abandoning your bicycle, and hide.'

'I will,' Rowan said. 'You can rest assured of that. And you?'

Oscar pressed a finger to his lips, and the kettle coming to a boil provided the dramatic effect.

'Need-to-know basis?' Rowan asked.

'That's a good way of putting it.'

Rowan prepared their tea and sat across from Oscar.

'Thank you,' Oscar said. 'What's weighing on your mind?'

The crease in Rowan's brow disappeared. 'You know who it is, don't you?' The question was barely more than a whisper.

Oscar glanced at the staircase, but David was undoubtedly not planning on leaving his library until it was time for the *apéro*.

'I might be wrong, Rowan.'

They contemplated the steam rising from their cups in silence.

'You need proof?'

'I'll be laughed at all the way out of the gendarmerie if I go to them with anything less than rock-solid proof.'

'Which you intend to obtain before daybreak tomorrow?'

Oscar nodded. 'If I'm not mistaken, I'll have evidence on at least one major point. Like I said, though, I could be wrong. That does happen to me once in a blue moon.' He winked.

'Who did you talk to during this walk of yours?' Rowan asked.

Oscar tapped his nose. 'Hold your horses, young man. You've been of great help so far and you'll be of even more before the case is cracked, but you and your father are my clients. You're not my colleague. Telling you more than you need to know would be a grave error of judgement, and might even put you in harm's way. Do you understand?'

137

'Has someone threatened me, Oscar? Wait a minute—you don't think—?'

'No, Rowan. Your father is the target—not you, but if Fred got in the way—well, it's best avoided, isn't it?'

Rowan nodded and sipped his tea.

'I'll tell you what I have to tell you and when I know it's the truth,' Oscar explained. 'You, on the other hand, have to tell me whatever I need to know to get the job done.'

'And I do.'

'I know you do,' Oscar said, glancing towards the staircase, and his point was taken by Rowan. 'Did you work on your studies?'

Rowan nodded.

'And you called your mother?'

'I did.'

Oscar sipped his tea, waiting for Rowan to elaborate, but he realised he'd have to prompt him.

'How did she react?'

Rowan sighed. 'She told me to come and stay with her and Tanguy while you sort it out.'

'She's worried about you?'

'Worried stiff. She was insistent.'

'But you refused,' Oscar said. 'You told her abandoning your father like that was out of the question, regardless of how difficult he could be.'

'That's right.'

'Is she also worried about him?'

'About Dad? Of course, but—'

'But he has to lie in whatever bed he's made for himself?'

'Basically. She told me to be careful.'

Oscar sipped his tea and remained silent.

'What's the matter?' Rowan asked.

'The matter is that I was wrong to ask you to participate in the investigation. There's always a chance it could all go wrong. I shouldn't have asked you to get involved.'

'There's no way I'm backing out, Oscar. I'll follow him, and like

138

you said, if he tries to turn the cart around and charge at me, I'll get off the track and hide. He won't though, will he? He can't afford to hang around for too long. The gendarmes will be here in a matter of minutes if anyone calls them and even mentions the name of the village.'

'I don't know, Rowan. If you get yourself killed—'

'I'm not going to get myself killed, Oscar. I plunged into a ditch once to save my skin. Escaping into the woods is a walk in the park in comparison, and while a scythe is a deadly weapon out in the open, you can't swing one in the woods.'

'Quite so. That's perspicacious of you. It's a promise then?'

'What's that?'

'Do you promise you won't get yourself killed?'

'I promise, Oscar.'

'That's enough for me,' Oscar said. 'In any case, I'll be right behind you. Now, what else did your mother tell you?'

He thought about it. 'She's been thinking about it, trying to figure out what's behind it all.'

'And?'

Rowan shrugged.

'She's had no sudden flashbacks of heated arguments and sworn enemies?' Oscar asked, half joking.

'Nothing like that. Dad's no stranger to arguments, but more of the sarcastic variety than the heated.'

'I see. What about your mother's partner, Tanguy—he doesn't want to punish him?'

'What for? No. I can't imagine Tanguy is connected to this.'

'He would have been on the boat with your mother last night, in any case.'

'He was,' Rowan confirmed.

'It seems I'm still fishing for motives, Rowan.'

'There's bound to be a fish somewhere in the murky waters.'

Oscar smiled and sipped his tea. 'Or perhaps fishing isn't the right analogy here. It might be more along the lines of hunting.'

'Hunting? Are you talking about the accident?'

Oscar studied Rowan's face. 'Has your mother talked to you about your father's archaeological pursuits?'

'Treasure hunting—is that what you mean?'

'It is, Rowan. Did she?'

'Yes,' Rowan said. 'She wonders whether it isn't connected to that.'

'But she doesn't have any particular suspicions?'

'No. How did you find out about that?'

'No comment for the time being. The real question is—why haven't you mentioned this before?'

Rowan sipped his tea to hide the look of guilt he'd failed to suppress.

'Oh, I get it,' Oscar said. 'Your dear mother wanted you to test me.'

Rowan nodded. 'Sorry. Between us?'

'Mum's the word. Tell me though, when did she suggest this?'

'Before I called you.'

'I thought so. She didn't tell you to be out with it now, in light of Fred's death?'

'She did,' Rowan admitted.

'But you wanted to find out whether I wouldn't dig it up myself?'

'I did—and you did after all. You passed the test.'

Oscar shot him an admonishing frown. 'No more tests, Rowan. It's too late for that. This is all coming to a head.'

'No more,' he said, placing his hand over his heart. 'But what could Dad's treasure hunts have to do with this? Did he strike gold?'

Oscar didn't say a word.

'You'd tell me?'

'I hardly could if he wouldn't. It's not my place to meddle in your personal affairs between father and son—well, not unless it is of immediate importance to solving the case. At any rate, the truth is that I simply don't know—not yet. But the picture is getting clearer, Rowan, and if my plan works, there'll be a whopping great spotlight pointed straight at it by morning.'

'What do you want me to do now? I can install the laser alarm again.'

Oscar considered telling him it wouldn't be necessary, but he changed his mind.

'I'll let you do that,' he said. 'Put your bicycle back into place behind the hedge while you're at it.'

'What then?'

'After that, you can go upstairs and see how your old man's doing. I'll need to give him his instructions and I want to have a look at his local history books.'

'You do?'

Oscar nodded but didn't elaborate.

Rowan walked to the kitchen window and looked outside to try to gauge how long it would be until sunset.

'Where's your car, Oscar?' he said, turning around.

'You want the Ankou to think you've left the village?'

Oscar nodded.

'It will be dark in a few minutes. If you get the alarm, I'll put it into place now.'

Oscar went upstairs and took the laser alarm from his duffel bag. He saw that the door to the library was closed. He knew David must have heard the floorboards creak a little, but he didn't come out of the room or call out to Oscar.

Once Rowan had left, Oscar went to the dovecote to fetch wood for the fire. It was then that he noticed, without a hint of surprise, that the cutting block was no longer exactly where he'd left it.

'You came back after all,' he said. 'No matter—I'll not forget what I saw, and now, you've told me how important it really is.'

He wrestled the cutting block away and checked inside the hole. It wasn't just the folded paper that had been taken, but the tea tin itself. Only the strip of tarpaulin remained.

Oscar put everything back into place and paused to think before carrying four logs back to the house. Why had the killer taken the battered old tin and not just the paper?

David was downstairs when Oscar entered the house.

'Thank you,' he said, helping Oscar with the wood. 'You must

141

think I'm a terrible client, locking myself away and carrying on with my writing. I've neglected you.'

'Not at all, David.'

'You did tell me to stay put, though, didn't you?'

'I did. You weren't disturbed?'

'By whom?'

'Your neighbours.'

'The gendarmes drew a crowd for a while, but everyone went home and locked themselves away eventually. Much like I did.'

'That's understandable.'

David prepared the fire and Oscar could tell he was deep in thought.

'You'll keep watch again tonight?' he asked eventually.

'He'll ride tonight, David. Make no mistake about it.'

'I heard you talking to Rowan. You have a plan?'

Oscar nodded. 'I do.'

'Rowan's taking part?'

'We all have our parts to play.'

'Yes.' David struck a match, but it didn't light. He tried again and it worked. 'He gets on my nerves sometimes, and I get on his, but he's my world—both of my children are.'

'Have you told your daughter about what's going on?' Oscar asked, even though he knew what the answer would be.

'Not on your life,' David said as the kindling caught fire.

'Rowan's determined to do his part, and his safety will be my first priority. You're the one I'm worried about.'

'I can take care of myself.'

'You can,' Oscar agreed. 'By staying inside and following the instructions I'm going to give you. I can't look after Rowan and you at the same time.'

'You're not here to babysit me,' David replied curtly. 'You're here to unmask the Ankou.'

'Agreed.'

'What do I do?'

'First of all, I want you to show me any books you have about the history of this area.'

'Why?'

'I don't believe a horse and cart can vanish into thin air,' Oscar replied. 'That's why.'

Understanding dawned on David's face and Rowan entered the house at that very moment.

'Rowan,' David said. 'Get the *apéritif* ready.'

'Of course, Dad.'

He turned back to Oscar. 'I know just the book you need.'

14. The Bedroom Window

'Is it useful?' David asked as he wandered over to the window overlooking the path.

'I think it will be.' Oscar continued flicking through the old hardback, pausing whenever he reached a book plate featuring an old aerial photograph or an even older sketch of a village and the surrounding marshland.

He flicked back and forth between images, comparing them.

'There used to be a track branching off the main path between Greno and Kergaillot,' Oscar said quietly, more to himself than to David.

'Is that a question?' David turned back from the window.

Oscar raised his head to meet his gaze. 'It's a statement of fact,' he said. 'At least, according to this book it is.'

'I haven't opened it in years, I'm afraid.'

'You don't explore the marshland all that often?'

'Not really,' David admitted. 'I certainly don't venture off the beaten track. Are you talking about the area shortly before Kergaillot where there's a small clearing to the right of the path, leading down to the water?'

'That's the very spot I'm talking about. What can you tell me about it?'

'Like you said, there used to be a track branching off from the clearing and following the edge of the marsh.'

'From the path, you'd turn right into the clearing, and then turn left before reaching the marsh to follow this track? Where did it lead?'

'I don't know,' David said. 'I didn't even realise it didn't exist any more. It hardly deserves to be called a track from what I remember.

144

It's all damp grass and probably often flooded. It was in all likelihood used by the locals to access the best reeds for thatching their cottages once upon a time.'

'Which means it was practicable for carts.'

'I suppose so. You've already had a look down there? Is it still accessible?'

'No,' was all Oscar said.

David walked slowly around the room, stopping when he reached the window again.

'Why are you interested if it's no longer there?'

It was an excellent question, of course, and Oscar only had one answer to offer.

'Because it has to be there. Nothing else makes an ounce of sense. Give me a minute, will you?' With that, Oscar closed his eyes and clasped his hands together over his nose and mouth.

David stared at the dolmen, which grew ever more otherworldly as the evening gloom gathered.

Rowan's footsteps sounded along the corridor.

'Ready for a drink?' he asked as he arrived in the library.

David shushed him.

'The Balvenie, aged in American oak?'

'Be quiet!' David snapped. 'Oscar's thinking.'

'What did you say, Rowan?' Oscar asked, opening his eyes.

Rowan glared at his father before turning to Oscar. 'I simply wanted to know whether you were both ready for an *apéro*, but there's no hurry.'

'*American oak*. That's what you said.'

'The Balvenie, aged in American oak.'

David and Rowan stared at Oscar, waiting for him to explain himself, but he was deep in thought, now stroking his moustache between thumb and forefinger.

'Oak,' he said quietly. 'Elm. Holly. Gorse.'

'I think you need that drink, Oscar,' Rowan suggested.

His remark was meant to lighten the atmosphere, but Oscar shot him a piercing glance and nodded vigorously. 'That's precisely what

I need.'

Downstairs, Rowan poured the drams and David stoked the fire.

'Fred did all your gardening?'

'Yes,' David said, taking a seat and raising his glass.

'Cheers,' they chimed.

'What's that got to do with the cart?' Rowan asked.

Oscar took a sip and smiled as the whisky's glow spread through his body. 'Everything,' he replied. 'Absolutely everything—unless I'm mistaken.'

'I checked,' Rowan said with a grin.

'Checked what?' Oscar raised his eyebrows.

'I checked the sky. There's no blue moon tonight.'

Oscar gave him a friendly punch on the arm and laughed.

'You're going to have to be a trifle more explicit with us, my dear fellow,' David said, and he was considerably calmer now he was enjoying a fine dram.

'It's no more than a flash of inspiration, but it's all I have to go on. Did Fred ever prepare the garden for a special event?'

'Like a birthday party or wedding reception?'

Oscar nodded. 'Anything like that?'

David's face was blank.

'I'm afraid we're not exactly the life of the village, Oscar,' Rowan told him.

'He may have done that for someone else in the area. I can't say.'

Oscar sipped his whisky.

'Do you think Fred helped the Ankou?' Rowan asked. 'That doesn't make sense.'

'Doesn't it?' He turned to David. 'We don't know why Fred was killed, do we?'

'No, we do not,' David said, trying—but failing—not to sound too blunt.

'I'm beginning to suspect that Fred's expertise was used by our killer. But it would have to be someone who was familiar with his work.'

'That doesn't narrow it down much, Oscar,' David said. 'Fred

146

worked for and with almost everyone in the area over the years.'

'That's what I thought.'

David drained his glass dry, and Oscar and Rowan exchanged a furtive glance. They could tell he was growing more nervous with every passing minute.

Oscar finished his dram and Rowan followed suit, then poured another round.

'What do you feel like for dinner tonight, Dad?'

'I'm not hungry.'

'Soup?' Rowan asked, and there was an aggressive edge to the question.

'Whatever you two want.'

'We should keep it light, Rowan. Not too many drams either.'

David stared into his glass before taking a sip.

The alarm receiver sounded and Oscar got up casually and headed for the stairs.

'Brieg,' David muttered.

'I know. Best check all the same.'

Oscar watched Brieg from the bedroom window, keeping back out of sight this time. The night promised to be a dark one, with heavy cloud cover and little moonlight—no bluish tint, as Rowan had pointed out.

Brieg had a torch with him this time, and he was using it to examine the scene, as though expecting to pick up clues the forensics team had overlooked. He wandered further towards the end of the path but stopped before reaching it and stood there staring at the cottages. Oscar fancied he could tell which one in particular was the focus of his attention.

'Brieg,' he confirmed when he returned downstairs.

'His usual self?' Rowan asked.

'Very much so,' Oscar replied. 'Only, he had a torch with him and used it to take a very good look at the dolmen.'

'He's not convinced the forensics team did a thorough job,' David scoffed. 'You two have a lot in common.'

'We do indeed,' Oscar said. 'I need to call home. I'll waltz down

147

to the bread oven. Won't be long.'

'No problem,' Rowan said.

'Right you are,' David added, and he glanced at the longcase clock.

Oscar put his jacket and cap on and left the house. He walked along the drive and stopped by the gateway. He observed the cottages, noting which had lights on, chimneys smoking, and cars parked out front. Fred Gaillo's home was the most notable in that it was completely dark.

Nobody was out and about, unless they were up at *Le Chêne*, but it would have been closed on a Monday evening.

Oscar called home to check that Louise and the boys were managing all right but kept an eye out for any activity while he spoke. He heard distant traffic on the road to Herbignac but nothing more. The village was dead quiet.

David was watching the BBC news when Oscar returned to the house and Rowan was pouring soup into a pot.

'Madame is holding the fort? David asked.

'All good,' Oscar replied.

'I've put some cream of mushroom soup on to simmer while we have a last dram,' Rowan said.

'Right you are,' Oscar told him, taking a seat and watching the evening news while his mind wandered. David was staring a little too intensely at the screen—his mind clearly elsewhere.

It was Rowan who eventually spoke, no longer able to hold his tongue.

'There are three of us here, and two of us know who it is and what lies at the heart of it all.' He tapped the soup spoon against the rim of the pot to reinforce his words.

David turned his head ever so slightly, as though unsure he'd heard someone knock at the door, before giving the television his undivided attention again.

Oscar offered Rowan a sympathetic smile but didn't speak.

'I feel so useless,' Rowan confessed.

David made a point of draining his glass—an act that only made his son more annoyed.

'I don't know for certain, Rowan. We've discussed this,' Oscar said quietly.

'*He* knows!'

David increased the volume.

'Really, Dad?' Rowan spat. 'You want to drown me out—that's your solution?'

'You don't know what you're saying, Rowan. Drop it!'

'We need to keep calm,' Oscar said. 'If we follow the plan, it will all be over by morning.'

'Look at him, Oscar! You see how nervous he is, don't you?'

Oscar shot Rowan a warning glance but it bounced straight off.

'He knows why this is happening, but he doesn't want us to know. His secret is about to be exposed and that terrifies him.'

David stood up and poured himself another whisky. 'What do you want from me, son?'

'I want you to stop thinking about yourself for a second!'

'Stop thinking about myself!' he boomed. He waved his arms to indicate the house around them, not caring that a good deal of whisky sloshed onto the floor. 'I'm thinking about *you*, Rowan—you and Alice.' He stopped himself from saying another word.

'Not now, Rowan,' Oscar pleaded. 'Let's all have some soup and let your father retire for the night. We can't appreciate how draining this is for him.'

Rowan bit his lip.

'I have to get back to my work,' David said. 'I'm not hungry. I'll let you two eat in peace.'

'You're running away,' Rowan said.

'Stop it, Rowan,' Oscar said. 'Please. Not tonight.'

'Maybe you deserve to be taken by the Ankou.'

'Rowan!' Oscar snapped, and it worked this time.

David took a sip of whisky and muttered something under his breath as he stamped up the stairs.

'That didn't help, Rowan. I'm deadly serious.' Oscar sighed. 'You shouldn't have said what you did.'

'I had to.'

'It wasn't the right time. Listen, we all need to stay in control tonight—especially your father.'

Rowan stirred the soup.

'It got too much—that's all. I'm sick of the secrets.'

'Naturally, Rowan,' Oscar said softly. 'I understand—I really do. There are answers I yearn for when it comes to my father. Answers I'll probably never have. You'll have yours very soon—'

'But?' he asked, reading Oscar's face.

'But you risk regretting it.'

Rowan walked to the coffee table. 'I need another one.'

'The last before we sup,' Oscar said. 'We can't fall asleep tonight. We'll leave your father to brood in the library, out of harm's way.'

'What could be so terrible he can't even tell his own son?'

Oscar didn't reply.

'It makes me wonder,' Rowan said.

'Wonder what?'

'Whether he didn't kill Fred himself—only I don't know why.'

Oscar stared into the fire to avoid Rowan's questioning gaze.

'Your father didn't kill Fred.'

'How can you be so sure?'

'The only time I heard him go downstairs was when he went to the toilet.'

'That's it? Rowan asked. 'That's the only reason. You must have slept a little.'

'Fitfully. But it's not the only reason.'

'What else then?'

'Your father wouldn't have beheaded Fred, left his body in the marshland, and left his head sitting on the dolmen. It doesn't fit his personality or his intellect. Even though he can be a rather cantankerous man, he wouldn't have gone about it that way. A man who is willing to risk irreparably damaging his relationship with his son to hide a secret isn't going to attract attention to himself by planting a severed head on a dolmen outside his bedroom window.'

Rowan sighed. 'Of course not.'

'Whoever killed Fred is hell-bent on torturing your father.'

'And has succeeded.'

'Yes,' Oscar said gravely. 'His first goal has well and truly been achieved. That's what concerns me most of all.'

Rowan understood. Tonight's act was to be the final one.

'But his reaction to Fred's death wasn't the same as everyone else's.'

'No, it wasn't,' Oscar agreed. 'He was perplexed and relieved.'

'He said he was relieved it wasn't me.'

'That's true, Rowan—but we both know it's not the whole truth.'

'I don't know anything, Oscar. You know and he knows. I don't.'

'For the moment, I *suspect*. When I tell someone I *know* something, it means I really do. Knowledge is not a notion to be bandied about and confused with opinion and sentiment. That, however, is not the sticking point here.'

Rowan nodded. 'Yeah, I get it—it's not your place to tell me.'

'It's his,' Oscar confirmed. 'That's what worries him. When the Ankou is exposed, it will all be dragged under the spotlight. There'll be no more dark corners for secrets to hide in.'

#

After a bowl of cream of mushroom soup with wholegrain bread and salted butter, Oscar suggested they get some rest while they could. He went to his room while Rowan stretched out on the sofa and watched television with the volume down low. Faint light seeping under the door to the library told Oscar that David was at work.

He entered the bedroom without switching the light on and looked out the window, but the darkness was impenetrable. The moon was veiled by thick clouds. He made his way to where he knew the bedside table to be and switched the lamp on, then checked his duffel bag to make certain all the tools of his trade were precisely where they should be. He plugged his phone in to recharge and placed it alongside the laser alarm receiver and his camera on

151

the bedside table. He put his torch and the Victorian-era police truncheon he'd bought for a steal that summer at an antiques market in Batz-sur-Mer on the floor beside his duffel bag.

The silence that reigned in Ker Greno was oppressive, but Oscar reminded himself it was an important tactical advantage. When the Ankou arrived on the scene, he wanted to hear the clopping of hooves and grinding of cartwheels before the laser alarm sounded. He wanted to be aware and in control from the very start of the act. In the meantime, he had to be calm and patient without falling asleep.

He put on his black tracksuit and a clean pair of black trainers and lay on the bed, contemplating the peculiar shapes made by the lamplight where it caressed the ceiling. Time ceased as he went over every detail of the case yet again, trying to identify where misinterpretation or supposition may have warped his reading of the affair.

Footsteps in the corridor roused him from his pondering shortly before ten o'clock. He listened as David went downstairs and returned a minute later. His footsteps stopped at the bedroom door and he knocked softly three times.

'Come in, David.'

He entered. 'Did I wake you?'

'Not a chance.'

'I'm turning in, Oscar.'

'Did you turn the light off in the library?'

'I did.'

'Excellent. We can't afford to put a foot wrong. How are you holding up?'

'Good, Oscar. Yourself?'

'I'm ready and waiting.'

'I'm counting on you. It's all in your hands now. Rowan is in your hands.'

'He won't be hurt on my watch. Rest assured. You know what to do when you hear the Ankou.'

'You've told me a dozen times,' he grumbled. 'I'm to stay in my room unless instructed otherwise.'

'Quite right,' Oscar replied. 'I'll let you get to bed, David. Good night.'

Without another word, David closed the door and retired to the guest room.

Oscar strolled from the bed to the window numerous times and went downstairs to use the toilet around a quarter to eleven. Rowan had turned the television off and put another log in the wood stove.

'Don't worry,' he said as Oscar passed him, looking to see whether his eyes were open. 'I'm wide awake. All quiet?'

'As the grave.'

'I'm ready to spring into action the moment that changes.'

Oscar went to the toilet and quickly returned to his room. He walked to the window and stared out into the darkness, and he was still there, engulfed in the void, when he heard his phone buzz.

He strode over to the bedside table and smiled as he read the single-sentence message he'd received. No sooner had he read it than he received a photograph. It was dark and taken from a distance, but he could see what was happening in it.

'You were spot on,' he congratulated himself.

He sent a reply of thanks and congratulations, and reminded the sender not to take further action. He then sent a message to Rowan, telling him to take his place by the bicycle.

Received loud and clear appeared on his screen a moment later.

This was it—the moment he'd been waiting for, and there was no room for error. David was in his room and Rowan would be on his way to the bicycle. Oscar checked that the lamp was just right and that his silhouette would be noticeable but not clearly distinguishable from the path once he was standing at the window. It was crucial the Ankou believed he was David.

He sat on the bed and waited to find out what would be the first warning of the Ankou's arrival, the alarm or the clopping of hooves and grinding of cartwheels.

As it turned out, all three sounds reached his ears at the very same moment in a ghastly disharmony. He waited for the cart to come to a halt by the dolmen before rushing over to the window the way a man suddenly disturbed from his sleep would be expected to do.

And there it was, that figure dressed in black, holding a cruel scythe in one hand, lamplight shining on the blade and the buckle of the broad-brimmed hat. The black horse stood still, patiently awaiting further instructions.

Oscar stared at the skull mask, into those unfathomable eye sockets. It was so realistic. He felt a shiver run through his body. He didn't doubt for a moment that a superstitious man couldn't help but believe it was the collector of souls in the flesh—well, so to speak—down there.

A gloved right hand raised the scythe into the air and there was a flash, as of lightning, as it made a slashing movement towards the window.

Oscar knew it was a risk, but it was one he had to take. He raised his hands with palms facing upwards and shrugged. David had probably never reacted in such a way, but before the Ankou disappeared into the night, Oscar wanted more than just a threatening gesticulation. One didn't go to all this trouble to haunt a man before killing him without making sure he knew why he had to die. In any case, Oscar was counting on that.

It turned out he was right. The Ankou rested the scythe against the nearest of the cart's lamp supports and reached down to what appeared to be a bag on the floor.

Oscar's mind raced, immediately discounting the terrifying prospect of yet another severed head, and yet, there was always that possibility. No—no that. This would be more personal—and as the Ankou straightened up, Oscar guessed what the object was a fleeting moment before the gloved hand held it up to the light coming from the nearest coachman's lamp. The Ankou knew that David Trevelyan would recognise it, even from so far away.

On that small battered tin, Oscar could make out a ghostly countenance he knew was that of Princess Diana. Her face seemed to shimmy under the flickering lamplight.

Oscar narrowed his eyes. In making this gesture, the Ankou was giving his identity away, knowing full well that his victim wouldn't go to the police. His gaze was still fixed on the tea tin when Oscar heard footsteps in quick succession followed by a sharp metallic sound coming from the corridor. He gasped and turned from the window, ready to stride over to his truncheon.

Did the Ankou have an accomplice who had somehow entered the house? Or had Rowan come back from his post for some reason? But it was neither of these explanations, was it? Just then, Oscar heard the door slam downstairs, and he understood what was happening.

'Stop!' he shouted. 'David!'

But it was too late for that. He grabbed the antique truncheon and his torch, flicking the latter on as he rushed into the corridor, and his fears were confirmed when he noticed that the sword was missing from the stand in front of the suit of armour. He hurried down the stairs and outside, and sprinted along the drive and around to the woodland path—hoping beyond hope that he wouldn't be too late to save his fool of a client.

15. The Sweep of the Scythe

Oscar rounded the corner of Ker Greno, his torch held steady in his left hand in a reverse grip and his truncheon hovering over his right shoulder. There was no shouting, but the black mare was stamping its hooves, and as the scene came into view, Oscar saw David take a swing at the dark figure towering over him. The blade struck the body of the cart, and before David could try again, the Ankou kicked out and the heel of its right boot landed on his forehead, sending him crashing against the wall of his house. Although it didn't look like the same boot, it was the very same blow Oscar had been dealt—only this time, it wouldn't end there.

'Get inside, David! Now! Think about your children!'

Both David and the Ankou turned to him, but it was the look on the professor's face that sent a shiver down Oscar's spine, not the impassive skull mask.

'Dad!' Rowan's voice boomed from the darkness beyond.

'Get back inside!' Oscar yelled, hoping David would come to his senses and listen to him—but he didn't. He raised his sword above his head with both hands and strode back to the cart.

Seeing that his father had no intention of retreating, Rowan came running along the path with the bicycle held over his head—Oscar knew he was planning on hurling it at the fiend.

It was now or never. Oscar didn't bother yelling at David again because he was clearly hell-bent on killing the Ankou or getting himself killed trying.

Oscar was about to dash around to the far side of the cart and climb onto the dolmen so he could use it as a siege engine. More or less level with the cart, he might be able to leap onto it and tackle the Ankou. With Rowan throwing the bicycle and Oscar attacking

156

from behind, they were bound to overpower him. All David had to do was keep his head out of the scythe's sweep.

But Oscar had to abandon his plan as he realised the very same idea had occurred to David. With speed and agility Oscar wouldn't have thought the professor capable of, David broke his stride and dashed to the left, passing between Oscar and the horse like a rugby player who'd just received the ball and was one sidestep away from a clear path to the try line. He reached the dolmen before either Oscar or Rowan could react to the change in tactic and climbed onto it as the Ankou turned around and raised the scythe. David made a downward slash and the tip of the blade cut into the sleeve of the Ankou's coat close to where the right elbow must have been. A loud grunt cut through the air, but the Ankou ignored the pain, took half a step backwards, and brought the scythe swinging down.

By this time, Oscar had reached the side of the cart facing the house and clambered halfway up. He was going to land a powerful blow of his truncheon on the back of the fiend's right knee in the hope of bringing him down to a position that would prevent him from using the scythe.

But he was a second too late. The cruel blade came swinging back up over the Ankou's left shoulder, and Rowan's harrowing scream tore through the night as drops of warm liquid landed on Oscar's face.

Rowan hurled the bicycle, but its trajectory was too low and it bounced off the cart. Oscar squinted to keep David's blood out of his eyes and swung his truncheon, but the Ankou kicked back blindly with his right foot and hit his target, making contact with Oscar's forehead and sending him tumbling to the hard ground.

With a whip of the reins, the horse and cart advanced into the village, and as Oscar got to his feet, he noticed that lights were flicking on behind those cottage windows that weren't hidden by shutters. It was too late though, the horse was now facing the path and the Ankou whipped the reins violently, making her charge.

There was nothing either Oscar or Rowan could do but leap out of the way as the Ankou hurtled past and disappeared into the

157

darkness.

Oscar wiped the blood off his face as best he could, dropped his torch and truncheon, and rushed over to Rowan. He placed a hand on either shoulder.

'Why didn't he listen to you?' he sobbed. 'The stubborn bastard!'

'He wanted the Ankou dead, Rowan. One of them had to die. I should have known he wouldn't stay put. If only I'd—'

'Locked him in his room?' Rowan shook his head. 'This is his doing. This is on his—' He didn't dare say that last word.

They were both staring at that dark round shape lying several feet from the dolmen. David's body lay crumpled where it had fallen at the foot of the dolmen. Thankfully, the scene was only faintly illuminated by the light from Oscar's torch.

'I hate to leave you like this, but I can't let the trail grow cold this time, Rowan. The police will already be on their way and the whole village will be out here before you know it.'

'Do whatever it takes to bring him to justice, Oscar. It's time to put an end to this. There'll be no more keeping of secrets now.'

Oscar grabbed his torch and truncheon, lifted the bicycle and checked that the wheels hadn't been buckled, then pedalled away along the woodland path. It wasn't easy going with only the torch to guide him. Its light shook as he rode as fast as he could along the uneven path, past where he knew Brieg's caravan to be. There was no sign of movement from the hermit. No lights.

Oscar peered ahead, hoping to catch a glimpse of the cart's two lamps swinging ghostlike in the air, but there was only impenetrable darkness beyond the reach of his torchlight.

When he reached the clearing on the right-hand side, he got off the bicycle and shone his torch at where he'd seen the cartwheel tracks in the ground. Discovering there were fresh tracks, as he'd expected, he switched the torch off and stood still for several seconds. He could hear movement nearby—hoofbeats—and then the black mare trotted past him and onto the path. It didn't stop or even acknowledge Oscar's presence, but simply made its way towards Kergaillot. It knew perfectly well how to get home on its own.

Oscar walked slowly through the clearing and stopped when he reached three holly bushes no higher than his chin. He dropped to his knees and paused again. No noise at all. The silence was eerie. Then, unless he was imagining it, he thought he heard the ever so faint sound of distant sirens. He got up, continued past the holly bushes—taking care not to let their prickly leaves catch his clothes—and still leaving his torch off, walked slowly through the stretch of long grass that separated the woods from the marshland. His truncheon was at the ready, but he knew his best bet for keeping his head would be to run into the woods if he caught sight of the Ankou. He was, however, quite certain there would be no encounter. The sirens were all too real and they were growing louder. The gendarmes would be in the village in a matter of seconds, and anyone not milling around the well or bread oven wearing a look of stunned disbelief, anger, or grief would be an immediate suspect.

Oscar was beyond the point of studying body language. His concern now was to gather overwhelming evidence to present once he'd filled in the few remaining gaps in the dark story he would have to share.

He could make out the cart through the grass. It was close to the curtain of reeds at the edge of the marsh. He switched the torch on as he drew nearer and was relieved to find that the only reaction was that of a large water bird taking flight nearby—a splash of water followed by the whoosh of broad wings in the air.

He swept the cart with his torch. The scythe was nowhere to be seen, but he'd have happily bet London to a brick the police divers would end up finding it in the marshes. The bag, on the other hand, sat on the floor of the cart.

'Why?' Oscar whispered to himself. Was it a foolish oversight or was the Ankou counting on coming back and disposing of it later, thinking the cart wouldn't be found?

He went through the motions in his mind. After the Ankou had unharnessed the horse and extinguished the lamps, he cast the scythe as far as possible into the marsh, and—? What then?

Oscar used his truncheon to carefully open the linen bag without touching it. He then shone his torch into it. The black hat, coachman's gloves, and long coat were in there. The skull mask and tea tin had also been left inside. There was one other item, which at first glance appeared to be a tub of hair gel or boot polish. He used the truncheon to push it to one side until the label was visible, and as he noted the logo and read the words, his lips formed a moustache-twitching grin.

He inspected the coat and found where the sword had bitten through. He raised the fabric to his nose. Blood—probably not much of it—but it would be enough.

He took the bag, walked back to the bicycle, and rode back to Greno.

#

Blue lights had invaded the village before Oscar made it back. He parked the bicycle by the hedge and slipped onto the grounds of Ker Greno. He deposited the bag in the old dovecote and hurried down the drive to where Rowan was being comforted by Thérèse Derrien and answering Major Faure's questions.

'I see you're still here, Oscar Tremont.'

'My work wasn't finished.'

'I'd say it is now,' the major said acidly.

Oscar knew better than to reply.

Rowan raised his eyebrows at Oscar.

'We'll catch him, Rowan. That's a promise.'

'The Gendarmerie Nationale will do everything we can to catch him,' Major Faure assured the bereaved young man. 'We don't make empty promises, but we get the job done. Now, Monsieur Tremont, were you trying to apprehend the assailant?'

'That was not my intention.'

'I told you,' Rowan cut in. 'My father went after him with a sword. Oscar and I tried to stop him.'

160

'He struck him on the left leg,' Oscar said, looking around as he spoke and making a mental note of who he could see staring curiously at them and along the path to where the gendarmes were once again cordoning off the scene. 'Is there blood on the sword?'

Major Faure merely huffed.

'Well, it's not my place to tell you how to do your job,' Oscar said. He hoped the major could complete the counterpart of the sentence in his head.

'My poor boy,' Thérèse said, giving Rowan's hand a squeeze. 'Whatever has happened to the world?'

'I don't know what he was thinking,' Rowan said quietly, and it was clear to see by the way he was staring at the ground that he was replaying the scene in his mind. 'How can such a clever man be so damned stupid?'

'We'll talk about that later, Rowan. For now, you need to take care of yourself,' Oscar told him. 'You'll need to decide how to break the news to your mother and sister in the morning.'

Oscar laid a hand on Rowan's shoulder while he surveyed the faces illuminated by the gyrating blue lights. There was Kevin, standing by the front door to his cottage, trying to keep his dogs from barking as he observed the commotion. Arnaud and Nina were outside their home, shaking their heads and explaining to the kids what was going on. Hervé and Denise were standing by the well, taking it all in. Bruno was hesitantly walking down the street as though undecided about whether he really wanted to know what had happened now. Brieg was nowhere to be seen, but that came as no surprise.

'Have you called Youna?' Oscar asked.

'I don't know whether I want to.'

'What do you mean?' Thérèse asked. 'You must. Can he call his girlfriend?' she asked the major.

'There's no reason why not. We've secured the scene and forensics will be back here soon. Everyone needs to try to get some rest. We'll talk in the morning.' He turned to Oscar. 'Monsieur Tremont—'

'Stay inside?' Oscar asked.

'Yes,' the major replied firmly.

'Loud and clear.'

'Thank you,' Rowan said to Thérèse. 'I'll be fine. I need to talk to Oscar alone.'

She frowned, but it promptly changed back to a comforting smile. 'You said you would pop by, Oscar. I don't have any herbal tea, but cognac makes for a fine nightcap.'

He shot her a wink before turning to Rowan. 'Let's go, young man.'

Rowan was scanning the village now, just as Oscar had been moments earlier.

'Not tonight, Rowan,' Oscar told him quietly. 'There's one piece left and then I'll have completed the puzzle. All will be revealed.'

He led Rowan along the drive, away from the staring eyes and flashing lights. He put another log in the wood stove and stoked the fire while Rowan poured himself a whisky—a double.

'I can't stay here all alone,' he mumbled.

Oscar knew it would drive him mad, living alone in the huge house. Youna would hardly want to move in either, not after the two brutal slayings. Ker Greno was stained.

'It's not the time to make plans, Rowan. It will be all too soon, but not tonight. Do you want to call Youna?'

'In the morning,' he said, dropping onto the sofa. 'Oh—I forgot—'

'I'll pour myself a dram in a minute. You need to look after yourself,' Oscar said.

'I'll call everyone in the morning.'

'That's a good idea,' Oscar said, closing the wood stove.

Rowan took a sip and looked up at him. 'You still won't tell me, will you?'

'It's not—'

'The time,' Rowan cut in, nodding. 'I don't know what terrifies me more—learning the identity of my father's killer or having his secret exposed.'

Oscar drew a deep breath and poured himself a dram. He sat next to Rowan and they raised glasses.

'To Dad,' Rowan said.

'To your father.'

'I wonder whether I ever really got to know him at all.'

'You knew him as much as he let you.'

'He should have let me know everything. I'm his son.'

'They're so closely entwined,' Oscar said sombrely.

'What are?'

'The identity of the Ankou and your father's secret.'

'When will you have the last piece, Oscar?'

'Tomorrow, I hope. I need to slip away early, before Major Faure has a chance to tie me up. If I haven't missed the mark by a mile, I'll have all the answers by nightfall. Would you be averse to letting me commandeer the dining room?'

'Are you telling me you want to gather everyone here to expose the murderer?'

'It would be convenient.'

'That would include the major.'

'It would, preferably with one of his best gendarmes by his side.' Oscar paused, weighing something up in his mind.

'What is it?'

'I was just thinking I should play it by the book for once.'

'*Play it by the book*?' Rowan repeated. 'That doesn't sound like you.'

Oscar took a sip of whisky before gazing at Rowan absently, as though giving that last comment some serious thought.

'No,' he said eventually. 'I suppose it doesn't. But this case hasn't quite turned out the way I'd planned.'

'Listen to me, Oscar,' Rowan said, his voice heavy not only with grief, but also with earnestness. 'This isn't your fault. My father went against your instructions, my pleading, and his own good sense—which is one of the qualities I most admired in him. Only two people are responsible for his death, unless I'm much mistaken.'

Oscar drew a deep breath, trying not to show his emotions. It was his reason he wanted to remain on display for Rowan.

163

'Thank you, Rowan.'

'I know you can't tell me what you intend to do in the morning, but can't you at least tell me why you're considering playing it by the book all of a sudden?'

'I won't be the one to place your father's killer under arrest, Rowan. That honour belongs to the gendarmes. I'm already pushing Major Faure's tolerance to the limit by failing to immediately disclose what I discovered tonight. Tomorrow, Rowan—bear with me a little longer. I'll tell you when I have all the pieces.'

'What exactly are you worried about?' Rowan asked.

'It's a balancing act. A private investigator can usually get away with "stumbling across" evidence while a police investigation is being carried out, but any suggestion that a crime scene has been contaminated can compromise a case, and in court, well, that can be the difference between a conviction and a mistrial.'

'The dolmen has been cordoned off again until the forensics team has processed the scene. You couldn't tamper with it even if you wanted to.'

Oscar stared into the fire. 'That's not the scene I'm talking about.'

Rowan sipped his whisky and listened to the crackling fire before speaking. 'Listen, Oscar, if you play it by the book and I make sure Major Faure appreciates your good will, it will work out in everyone's interests. That's how I see it.'

'I do hope so,' Oscar said. 'It depends on him.'

'Do what you need to do tomorrow and call or message me as soon as you have the last piece to the puzzle. I'll do whatever I can to convince the major to listen to you. What do you think?'

Oscar nodded, turning from the fire to Rowan. 'I think that's the best way to go about it. What do you keep in the garage?'

'What—why?'

'It's important,' Oscar assured him.

'The cars, of course,' Rowan said. 'We keep a few other bits and bobs there as well. There are tools and beach equipment—that kind of thing.'

'Tools for what sort of work?'

Rowan shrugged. 'I don't know exactly. There's a hammer and a saw, and a tyre jack and jump leads.'

'No gardening or building tools, I guess, since Fred looked after all that?'

'Not a whole lot. I think there must be a gardening fork, a rake, and a hand spade.'

Oscar nodded. 'What can I do for you?'

'Now?'

'Yes, now.'

'I don't know. Nothing at all. I'll have another dram after this one and then try to get some sleep—or at least lie in bed. I'll call my mother in the morning, and then I'll call my sister, unless mum wants to do it for me.' He shrugged. 'All I ask of you is to lay your hands on that last piece.'

16. The Last Piece of the Puzzle

It was still dark when Oscar crept downstairs with his duffel bag, determined not to disturb Rowan from the slumber he hoped had eventually claimed him. Ker Greno felt different now. The sword missing from the suit of armour seemed to represent David's sudden absence. The house was somehow lighter and more solemn at the same time. Oscar felt like damning David to hell for getting himself killed, but that made no sense. In any case, even if he were a religious man, he'd be inclined to suspect David's soul would stay put right here in Ker Greno, for evermore staring down at the dolmen from his bedroom window.

He put his jacket and flat cap on and headed outside, opening and closing the door as quietly as possible. It was a chill morning and the ground wasn't overly damp. Dawn was still a good forty minutes away.

He had observed the forensics team at length from the window before going to bed and had noticed when he woke from his sleep around three o'clock that they were no longer at the scene. He suspected Major Faure would be back in the village around nine o'clock to take full statements from the villagers.

He went to his car and put his duffel bag on the passenger seat, but before sitting in the driver's seat, he took his torch and used it to guide him to the dovecote to fetch the Ankou's linen bag. He put the bag in a spotlessly clean cooler in the boot where it would be safe from the prying eyes of the gendarmes until he was ready to reveal the murderer's identity. He then went to the garage and found a plastic bucket and a hand spade. He put them in the boot, sat behind the wheel, and turned the key in the ignition. After giving the motor a minute to warm up, he drove out of Greno—the soft

166

glow of his vintage car's humble headlights struggling to cut a path through the infinite darkness.

He turned left at *Le Chêne* and left again at the road from Guérande to Herbignac. He knew where he was driving and where he would park, and he had a fairly good idea which way he would have to walk after that and through which type of terrain, but there were no guarantees he'd find what he was as close to sure as he could be was out there.

Once Oscar was on the main road, he turned the radio on and went through channel after channel of unbearable talk shows and pop music until he heard the unmistakable voice of David Bowie singing about life on Mars. Oscar didn't know much about the inhabitants of other planets, but since returning from Australia, his understanding of the strangeness and mystery that was an intrinsic part of rural life in Brittany was coming along in leaps and bounds. Unravelling the complexity of coexistence in what to outsiders looked like a peaceful, idyllic village was an art form all of its own. In cities, you could avoid people and melt into the masses, but in a village like Greno—with the same narrow street bringing you in and leading you out, and the ancient well the focal point, like a spotlight aimed at centre stage—there was no going unseen. No way, Oscar thought, except by wearing a mask—but a mask was also a face, wasn't it? That, in a way, was the last piece of the puzzle.

There were only lorries on the road at that time of morning and their headlights were almost blinding, but they were few and far between. Oscar kept his attention on the road. One of his wife's colleagues had run into a boar not a week ago and the impact had caused considerable damage to his car. Oscar avoided using his car to do the grocery shopping and parked in a secluded spot far from the main entrance when he had no choice. The thought of a shopping trolley leaving a dent or scratch in its flawless black paintwork made his skin crawl, so how he'd react if a boar decided to sprint across the road and get itself killed didn't bear thinking about.

But he arrived in Herbignac without incident and drove along

167

softly lit streets and through two roundabouts until he returned to a country road again. He followed it until the headlights exposed the entrance to a car park—a gateway beyond which was only darkness. A hint of daylight, however, now touched the sky.

He stayed in the car but turned the radio off, not wanting to let the battery run flat, and judging by what he'd been listening to for the last few minutes, it seemed David Bowie was the highlight of the morning playlist. The instant it was light enough to make his way about, he'd leap into action. He could have done with a thermos of herbal tea and would have made himself one if he hadn't wanted to risk rousing Rowan so early. He wasn't a child, but losing your father—however old you are and however difficult the man may have been—was always painful. The only consolation—cold comfort under the circumstances—was that Rowan knew exactly what had happened. His father hadn't disappeared into thin air, or a puff of smoke. He knew his father had been killed trying to hide a secret, and he was only hours away from learning the nature of that secret and the identity of the murderer. He had to be told, whether he wanted to or not. Justice, Oscar knew, was a hungry hatchling that wouldn't be satisfied until its belly was full. The job of a private investigator was to discover the truth and represent his client's interests in so far as that didn't place the investigator at odds with his own conscience, and—officially at least—the law. Rowan was Oscar's sole client now, and only David's reputation could be—and had to be—called to account.

He stretched his arms and looked through the windscreen to contemplate the faint pinkish glow that was making the twigs and leaves of the trees separating the car park from the picnic area more distinguishable by the minute. His mind then turned to the task at hand. He didn't have a map, but he could picture where he had to go. It would just be a matter of getting there and identifying the site. Well, maybe. It was simple enough in theory, but not necessarily in practice. Oscar remembered all those times bushwalking and camping back in Queensland. Once he and Louise had become parents, they'd slowed down, but back when it was just the two of them, he'd often convinced her to take shortcuts off the beaten track, using a map and compass to guide them. There were times when they'd had to do an about-turn after running into a sheer drop at their feet or a cliff face rising in front of them, and the shortcut had sometimes ended up turning into an arduous detour. On those occasions, Louise hadn't always finished the day talking to him, even though he'd never failed to point out that every extra step was one closer to them both having perfect buttocks. But this was Brittany, not Queensland, and he reckoned the walk from the car to the grotto to be no great deal further than from where he parked his car when he went to the supermarket and the fresh produce section. He wouldn't get lost, let alone bitten by a venomous snake, and the pair of wellies he kept in a plastic bag in the boot would keep his feet reasonably dry.

It was almost dawn now, so Oscar got out. He took his duffel bag from the passenger seat, checked that he was alone, and walked around to the rear of the car to open the boot. He took his Doc Martens off and pulled his wellies on, then took the bucket and hand spade before closing the boot again.

He switched his torch on as he crossed the car park and started through the picnic area. There was a house beyond a high wall to his left but no windows were visible. To his right was a crumbling stone wall with patches where breaches had obviously been filled in during renovations over the years. The top of the wall was uneven and there were curtains of ivy hanging down at irregular intervals along its length.

Keeping the torch pointed at the ground, Oscar followed the outer wall, hugging it closely as much as possible but giving it a wider berth wherever a tangle of brambles or a copse of trees blocked him. The chill air was surprisingly pleasant and refreshing, and it occurred to him that it was probably a more effective way of kick-starting the day than sipping a mug of herbal tea. He often went for a morning jog when the occasion arose, but this was the first time in a while he'd ventured into the woods at the crack of dawn.

Once the sun was high enough to provide sufficient natural light for him to see where he was going, he switched his torch off but didn't put it away in his duffel bag. It came in handy to push branches to one side. After he'd been weaving his way for three or four minutes, the wall curved to the right, leaving Oscar facing sparse woods where speckled sunlight formed a patchwork on the rough ground. He walked carefully, avoiding ditches wherever necessary. Under the surface lay the ruins of bygone eras.

When he noticed a grassy knoll to his right, he remembered a symbol he'd seen on the map and knew it was the only feature in the landscape that could correspond. He walked around it and followed the gentle slope that led downhill. The woods grew thicker here and he had to look around for a way through the undergrowth. There had to be a well-worn track, for if there wasn't, it meant he'd been wrong, and that was an unbearable prospect. Louise took it upon herself to remind him no one was infallible whenever he happened to come to a false conclusion—and that was a habit he encouraged—but to be so completely off the mark was unthinkable.

He breathed a sigh of relief that sent a cloud of vapour rising into the air when he saw exposed earth and a narrow gap in the undergrowth. He approached that point, stopped, and crouched. There were shoeprints in a patch of soft ground that had escaped being covered with leaves, and they were remarkably clear. He flicked the torch on and examined them but could only speculate as to whether the pattern he saw was from one of the two soles that had struck his head.

He reminded himself to count his lucky stars—he still had his head. A boot or two to the head was a sight better than the well-aimed swing of a scythe to the neck.

He reached into his jacket pocket and used his phone to take pictures of the prints from several angles. He checked that they were perfectly clear, then stood up. After stepping over the exposed patch of ground, he continued into the woods, where a carpet of leaves squelched under his wellies. Determining which way to go wasn't so easily done now. Unlike fields, woodlands were subject to

170

constant change—leaves and branches falling, saplings springing up, and creepers and climbers spreading out and up and over, covering whatever they could. What Oscar needed to find was another dip in the landscape, and this one would be almost entirely protected by a ring of rocks and thickets.

He passed an ancient oak and stepped over a fallen elm, then kept walking around until he kicked something hard that jarred his toes through his wellies and thick socks made of Merino wool from the homeland. Looking down, he saw a mossy rock sticking out of the ground, and there were others to either side of it. In front of him, distinguishable now he knew what he was seeing, was a wall of gorse and holly.

Oscar worked his way slowly to the left, working himself, his duffel bag, and the bucket through tight squeezes as he progressed. He stopped when he came to an opening that could only be manmade. The branches had been hacked back, leaving a gap only wide enough to be passed through by turning sideways. He placed the bag and bucket on the ground, slipped through the gap, and reached out again to lift them inside. He turned to peer into the small but deep hollow, and he immediately recalled those distinctive holes made by artillery shells he'd seen on a visit to First World War battlefields in Flanders. At the bottom of this hollow, hidden behind a makeshift screen of branches, he found a rusty gate protecting a grotto no bigger than the average domestic oven.

A chill ran through his body as he clambered down. The last piece of the puzzle was now in place.

On the other side of the gate was a metal toolbox that had once been dark green but was now mostly a hotchpotch of rust and dirt. A small padlock kept it locked and a chain connected the handle on the top to a thick root that looped down from the roof of the grotto. On either side of the toolbox sat a saucer, each of which held the ghostly remains of one white candle that had already be used for hours on end.

Oscar clasped his hands together over his nose and mouth. He contemplated the gate for a moment, then closed his eyes and went for a stroll in his mind's eye.

When he opened his eyes again, he reached into his duffel bag and rummaged around until he found a pair of latex gloves and his bolt cutters.

Major Faure was going to have to find it within his heart to forgive this one last transgression. All Oscar needed was a single confirming glimpse and he promised himself he'd call Rowan.

He carefully lifted the gate away, snapped the padlock, and lifted the lid.

One glimpse was enough. He didn't even allow himself the pleasure of a victorious moustache-twitching smile. He merely closed his eyes and shook his head as Sir Walter Scott's words about tangled webs came to mind.

#

'How are you doing, Monsieur Trevelyan?'

'I'm keeping it together. Thank you, Major Faure.'

'I am very sorry to have to disturb you so early at what I know is a difficult time, but I'm afraid I have some further questions to ask you.'

'Do come inside,' Rowan said. 'Can I offer you some coffee?'

'I've had plenty already this morning,' the major replied, looking around the kitchen and living area inquisitorially.

'Are you able to shed any light?' Rowan asked, indicating for him to take a seat.

'Forensics are processing the scene and—'

'Performing the post-mortem,' Rowan said, nodding solemnly.

'You mentioned last night that the sword was your father's.'

'Yes, but he'd never, well, *used* it before.'

'I don't suppose he had. He struck a formidable blow though and there's a chance we'll find the culprit's DNA on the tip of the blade.'

'That's it then—case closed?'

'I'm afraid it's not that simple. We can't oblige everyone in the village to provide a DNA sample. We need evidence to—'

Rowan's phone started to vibrate and the major narrowed his eyes. Rowan picked it up and answered.

'Oscar Tremont?' Major Faure mouthed the question.

Rowan nodded.

'Did I not tell him to stay inside last night?'

Rowan listened to Oscar and then passed on his reply, translating it into French as he did so. 'He says he left Ker Greno this morning, thereby not going against your instructions—' He listened. 'Instructions that he informs me are not legally binding anyway. You have no authority to impose a curfew on a law-abiding adult.'

'Law-abiding?' The major huffed.

Rowan grinned.

'What's he saying now?'

'He has rock-solid evidence against the murderer of my father and Fred Gaillo.'

Rowan tried to keep a straight face as he watched the major's turn red.

'Any information pertinent to an investigation currently being carried out by the Gendarmerie Nationale must be—'

'Yes, yes, he's saying—he has every intention of handing the evidence over to you and allowing you to take official credit for the apprehension of the culprit. However, he requests that you indulge his whimsical sense of the dramatic by allowing him to reveal the identity of the murderer in his manner.'

Rowan allowed himself a faint smile as he saw the major relax. His epaulettes dropped a fraction of an inch and the ruddiness drained from his cheeks.

'Do you want to talk to him directly?' Rowan asked.

'No,' the major said sternly. 'You're doing well, Monsieur Trevelyan. When?'

'This evening,' Rowan said. 'Here at Ker Greno.'

Major Faure stared at Rowan's phone. 'He wants you to invite your father's murderer into your home?'

'This is no longer my home,' Rowan informed the major. 'My

173

mother is on her way here at this very moment. My sister will come as soon as possible, for my sake, and because we need to make some big decisions together. Regardless of what we decide, I'll be leaving the village.'

'Perfectly understandable,' the major said quietly. He glanced around the kitchen before turning back to Rowan, and frowning.

'What is it?'

'Oscar Tremont has quite a reputation. If what I've heard is true, I don't doubt he's got the whole case neatly wrapped up.'

'I have every confidence in him,' Rowan admitted.

'Is he still on the line?' Major Faure asked.

'Oscar?' Rowan listened. 'Yes—I'll tell him.' He nodded at the major. 'He heard every word you said.'

'Whose attendance does he request?'

'Everyone?' Rowan asked.

'He wants everyone in Greno to come?' the major asked wide-eyed.

Rowan listened, then rattled off a list of names that covered almost everyone in the village.

'We'll do what we can,' the major said.

'Oh, and he needs Jessica Chotard to be there.'

'Anyone else?'

'I don't know,' Rowan told Oscar. 'Major, do you know if Barbara Gaillo is coming back soon?'

'I don't think so. She's staying with her parents. We've sent our people to interview her.'

'He says her presence isn't essential.'

'I'd like to speak to him in person as soon as possible,' Major Faure said.

Rowan listened. 'He'll be back in twenty minutes, but he needs you to send out a forensics team.'

'What?' the major practically spat.

'I'll tell him, Oscar. So, the thing is, Major Faure—he doesn't want to tamper with the scene and risk compromising evidence.'

'I should hope not! He has found more evidence?'

174

'Yes,' Rowan replied. 'He found more evidence this morning.'

'What it is?'

'He says you're asking the wrong question.'

'What? Oh, all right, *where* is it?'

Rowan repeated the location Oscar gave him and shrugged at the look of bewilderment the major shot him.

'What's that, Oscar?' Rowan spoke into the phone. 'Oh—yes, *completely.*'

'What's he saying?' the major snapped.

'He wanted to know whether you looked perplexed.'

Major Faure grunted. 'I'll send forensics,' he said. 'Tell him he'd better not leave any loose ends untied.'

Oscar had heard him, and Rowan was about to repeat the investigator's reply about handing the major a neat package with a ribbon, but Major Faure had already taken his leave.

17. Invitation to Ker Greno

Thérèse and Denise were standing by the well, pretending not to be waiting for Major Faure, who had parked a far from inconspicuous gendarmerie Renault by the hedge. They couldn't possibly have failed to notice his creased brow and pursed lips, but fat chance that was going to put them off.

'Good morning, Major,' Thérèse chirped, in that charming little-old-lady way she'd made a point of mastering.

He nodded politely and greeted them but made a beeline for his vehicle.

'Oh, Major,' Denise took over, her tone drier than her elderly neighbour's. 'Any news?'

He stopped at the door to his Renault and turned to them, trying not to appear impatient or unpleasant, while aiming not to seem too friendly either. He opened his mouth to speak, then snapped it shut again as he decided what to say.

'I'm afraid we are not in a position—'

'Oh,' Thérèse said loudly. 'That's so official sounding, isn't it, Denise? We just want to know if we're safe.'

He drew a deep breath. 'There's no need to worry. This has nothing to do with you.' He instantly regretted those words.

'Nothing to do with us?' Denise gasped, shooting an incredulous glance at Thérèse. 'We are all simply terrified! If the Gendarmerie Nationale can't be trusted to make us feel safe, who can be?'

'Of course. What I mean to say is—' He cleared his throat. 'There is no reason to fear for your own safety.'

'He knows something,' Thérèse said quietly to Denise. 'That means he has information—'

'I do need your help, however,' Major Faure said, knowing that

176

would get their attention—especially Thérèse Derrien's.

'What could *we* possibly do?' Thérèse asked, wide-eyed.

'We are requesting everyone's attendance at a meeting this evening in Ker Greno.' He spoke as though he had a bitter taste in his mouth. 'We will be in a position to provide you all with further details regarding the investigation at this time.'

Thérèse and Denise exchanged a glance.

'Oh, I see,' Thérèse said, letting the last word hang. 'By *we*, you mean, in fact, *Oscar Tremont.*'

Major Faure didn't respond.

Denise was frowning. 'Has the private investigator identified the killer?'

'Everyone here at seven o'clock this evening,' the major all but snapped. But he immediately regained his composure. 'Can you help me with that?'

'Consider it done,' Thérèse agreed enthusiastically.

The major climbed into the Renault and closed the door loudly behind him.

Once he'd driven out of the village and the two women were wondering whether to go and talk to Rowan—to offer to make him some tea or coffee, or whatever little gesture they could make to ensure he was holding up—a bicycle came speeding along from the woodland path. It was Youna. She was wearing a khaki jacket and her blonde hair was tucked into a red wool bonnet. She seemed to hesitate for a moment, then made up her mind and headed over to the two women. She got off her bicycle and rested it against the stonework of the well.

'Hello, Youna,' Denise said with a mournful smile before nodding in the direction of Ker Greno, whose walls glowed feebly under the faint morning light behind a thin veil of cloud. 'How is he?'

She shrugged. 'I don't know. I heard the news from Jessica Chotard just now. I think her father found out early this morning. You know what farmers are like—up early and doing the rounds. Rowan didn't call me.' She glanced at the manor with concern. 'I

177

tried to call him as soon as I finished talking to Jessica and could get a signal, but he didn't answer.'

'The poor young chap,' Thérèse mused. 'We were just asking ourselves whether we ought to go and check on him. He's just had a visit from Major Faure of the gendarmerie.'

'Oh,' Youna said, a little surprised. 'Well, I suppose that's only to be expected,' she added a moment later. 'Is the investigator with him? Jessica mentioned him.'

'Yes—' Thérèse began, but then looked at Denise, who shrugged. 'Oh, well, I'm not sure.'

'Major Faure didn't say so,' Denise said. 'But he did inform us there would be a public meeting this evening and that everyone's attendance is strongly requested.'

Youna frowned. 'Everyone who?'

'He didn't specify,' Denise replied. 'Everyone in the village, I think.'

'In Greno?'

'I'm certain he wouldn't object to you being present, Youna, even though you're from Kergaillot,' Thérèse said. 'He probably expects you to be there.'

'No one will stop me from being with Rowan—except he himself,' Youna asserted, and the strength of her words stirred something inside the two older women.

'Young love,' Denise mused. 'Cherish it, my girl—cherish it!'

Youna smiled and did her best to stop a tear from welling in her eye.

'This meeting will take place in Ker Greno?'

'Yes,' Thérèse said. 'At seven o'clock.'

Youna bit her bottom lip. 'That's not usual protocol.'

'Not at all,' Thérèse said. 'I'm proud to say I've had little to do with the police in my life, but they're generally tight-lipped and share as little as they can with the public. Oscar is behind this. There's no doubt about it.'

'That can only mean—' Youna began.

The women nodded. 'All will be revealed tonight,' Denise said.

178

'The major wouldn't be letting a foreign private detective pull the strings without good cause, would he?'

The ensuing silence confirmed their agreement.

'Get along and see him now, Youna,' Thérèse said.

She got on her bicycle and rode up the drive.

'That's interesting, isn't it?' Thérèse asked. There was a hint of mischief in her voice.

'What's that?' Denise asked.

'Youna said Jessica asked about Oscar.'

'I don't follow.' Denise's face was blank.

Thérèse hummed thoughtfully. 'It might be nothing.'

'Come on, Thérèse—you've never been one to let the cat get your tongue.'

Thérèse narrowed her eyes. 'If the girl asked about Oscar, that means they've spoken to each other.'

Denise nodded. 'And?'

'What would he talk to her about?'

'I don't know, Thérèse—anything.'

'Anything?'

'With that girl, most likely about horses,' Denise said, and she laughed—but then she fell silent, having realised what she'd said.

#

The last thing Oscar wanted to do was sit around waiting for forensics to arrive. The police and gendarmerie belonged to the monolithic world of French bureaucracy, so there was no telling how long they'd take to get there. He had no choice though, because they would need him to lead them to the grotto.

While he waited, he strolled around the site. The mystery that had enshrouded the landscape before dawn was gone now in the cloud-filtered daylight. He walked along the walls, touching the rough stonework here and there, and he stopped to admire the masonry in the sections that had been renovated.

He walked slowly, playing out the coming evening's performance

179

in his head and letting the tranquillity of his surroundings fill him. There was no one else around, although he noticed there was one other car now, parked just inside the entrance to the car park. It was also a Peugeot—a burgundy hatchback, modern and in good condition, but completely charmless compared to his 403. It wasn't a vehicle he recognised from Greno or Kergaillot. He stopped and considered it. He hadn't been followed, had he? It seemed unlikely. He would have noticed headlights behind him in the dark, and no one knew he'd come here. He wondered who it could be.

A grating sound came from the other side of the stone wall. It echoed through the quiet air. A metal door being opened, or shutters.

'Of course,' he said aloud. The summer high season was well and truly over, but there were still tourists in Brittany in late October— the ones who preferred the risk of bad weather to crowds of Parisians on holiday. Oscar completely understood them. It was at this time of year that retired Germans in luxury motorhomes were on pilgrimage here. The historic site was still open for a week or two. Since he was stuck here, he figured he'd may as well pop in and have a look around.

Out of habit more than anything else, he peered into the car as he strolled past but saw nothing except a small stuffed panda on a child's seat in the rear and what looked like a pirate romance novel accompanied by a hairbrush on the front passenger seat. He kept going, following a gravel path past a well and a seesaw to his right and an apple tree and information panels to his left. He then arrived in a gravel courtyard where a gatehouse with a thatched roof served as ticket office and boutique.

'Good morning,' he greeted the woman inside. She was a few years his junior, probably in her thirties, and her brown hair appeared to match the strands he'd spotted on the brush in the car. She looked up at him, eyebrows raised over amber eyes.

'Good morning, and welcome. Would you like to visit the site?'

'I haven't decided,' Oscar replied. 'I've been here before, you see, and I was just walking around, stretching my legs.'

'I understand,' she lied, being polite.

He was usually much better at making up stories and suspected the rather charming woman had disarmed him.

'Is that black Peugeot yours, if you don't mind me asking?'

'Oh, no—I mean, yes, it's mine. I don't mind you asking.'

She suppressed a laugh.

'A beautiful car.'

'Thank you. She requires a lot of care and attention.'

'I'm sure she's worth it though.'

'Oh, absolutely.'

He looked around the boutique, almost feeling guilty for wasting her time, but there was no one else around. There were brochures and posters advertising events of all kinds, from markets and concerts to puppet shows and basket workshops, but they were all past events—July and August mostly, with one or two dated September. Of the one or two, one in particular caught Oscar's eye and got him thinking.

'That antiques market in September...' he began.

'Yeah, it was a pleasant day.'

'You were there?'

'Yes,' she answered. 'Why?'

There was a chance he was going to have to come clean. At any rate, she was bound to start asking questions once forensics invaded the car park.

'I'm interested in antique farming tools.'

He walked over to the poster. It showed pitchforks, bridles, cartwheels, a plough, and a man dressed up as a scarecrow—which struck Oscar as being both out of keeping and a tad disturbing.

'The market's held at the same time every year.'

'I wonder whether there were any scythes,' he said, not framing it as a question.

She took the bait. 'Quite a few. I sold one myself.'

He pretended to read the poster again. 'Oh, you're a member of the folk association? Well, it only stands to reason.'

'Do you collect farming antiques?' she asked, and he could tell

181

she was daring him to lie.

'No,' he admitted. 'I should tell you who I am.'

She looked at him expectantly.

'I'm a private investigator.'

Her surprise was genuine. 'That's exciting! From Belgium?'

'No, that hard-to-place accent belongs to an Australian.'

'Oh, I was miles off. Sorry.'

'Quite a few miles off, and in the wrong direction.' He winked. 'No need to apologise. I may not be Belgian, but I'm partial to their beer, so I'll take it as a compliment.'

'Your French is excellent.'

'Thank you.'

'Are you on a case—?' Her question faded and her jaw dropped as it dawned on her. 'The murder in Greno!' she gasped.

'You've heard,' he said.

'Everyone has heard. A man's head was found on a dolmen. They say it was the—' She paused, not wanting to speak that dreadful name, but she immediately shook the superstition off her shoulders—'the Ankou.'

She hadn't heard about the second death yet, and Oscar wasn't going to be the one to tell her.

'Do you know the person you sold it to?'

She shook her head.

'If I showed you a picture, do you think—?'

'It's worth a try.'

Oscar fished his phone out of his pocket and brought up the Facebook profile of the person in question. He enlarged a clear profile picture and held his phone up for her to see.

She turned her gaze from the phone to Oscar and nodded.

'You'd swear to it?'

She hesitated. 'Will it come to that?'

'I don't know.'

She nodded again. 'If need be.'

'Payment was made in cash?'

'I don't remember—almost certainly.'

'It doesn't matter. Your word will be enough, if it's needed. Like I said, I don't know that it will be. Chances are it won't.'

'Why is that? Is there other evidence?'

'There most certainly is, and if I pull it off this evening, the gendarmerie will have a full confession handed to them on a silver platter.'

'How thrilling!' she hissed. 'To think I've touched the murder weapon.' She shivered, and not entirely involuntarily, it seemed to Oscar.

18. Mum's the Word

'You really ought to have a little, Rowan,' Youna said, picking at the simple salad of tinned tuna, rocket, and parmesan that she'd whipped up.

But he wasn't hungry. He was sipping his tea and staring out the kitchen window as though mesmerised by the salt cedar.

'Later—' he said without looking at her. 'I'll eat later.'

'I almost don't want to know,' she confessed, stabbing her fork into the rocket leaves and twisting it to catch flakes of tuna and parmesan.

He turned to her and smiled faintly. 'I can understand that, but for my part, I need to know. Whoever it is and whatever the reason, I need to know.'

It was then that the sound of tyres on gravel reached their ears.

'Oscar's back?' Youna asked.

A white Citroën sedan came into view and stopped by the salt cedar.

'Not Oscar. It's my mum.' He got up and walked to the door. 'Alone.'

Anne got out of the car. She was dressed simply in jeans that did justice to her fine figure and a pink and white Breton stripe top. She had a small overnight bag with her, making it unclear how long she intended to stay. Rowan supposed it depended on him.

'Hi, Mum.'

They exchanged kisses on each other's cheeks and stepped inside. Anne looked around as though she no longer recognised the grand home where she'd spent so many years. Her perusal ceased when she saw Youna.

'Hello, Madame Trevelyan.'

Rowan laughed.

'What?' she asked, then at seeing the blank look on Anne's elegant face, realised her mistake. 'Sorry'

'No need to apologise, Youna,' Anne reassured her. 'Just don't ever call me that again, for heaven's sake.' She smiled warmly. 'Call me Anne. It's my fault, of course, for not coming here more often, but—' she cut herself short.

'I understand,' Youna said.

'You should come and see the boat sometime, Youna,' Rowan said, and he gave his mother a meaningful glance. '*Bleiz Mor* is a gorgeous vessel.'

'Oh, yes—we'll do that as soon as all this is sorted. I tend to get lost in my own little world.' She put her bag down on the floor. 'How are you both? I've been worried sick.'

'We're fine, Mum. It will all be over soon.'

'All over this evening, if our investigator is to be believed?'

Rowan nodded.

'Have you had lunch, Anne?' Youna asked.

Anne smiled at hearing her use her first name. 'Yes, I had a bite on the road. I wouldn't say no to a cup of black coffee though.'

Rowan filled the kettle.

'I'm so sorry for you, Rowan. I couldn't stand the man—I know I shouldn't talk like that, Youna, but I suppose Rowan has told you the whole story—but I'm sorry for you. No child deserves that. You and your sister don't deserve that.'

'Have you heard from Alice?'

'She won't make it here tonight.'

'Maybe that's for the best,' Rowan said. 'But we're not children now, Mum. I'm not a little boy.'

'No, of course not, but you'll always be his son.'

'I'll miss him.' He drew a deep breath. He didn't want to do this, especially not in front of Youna.

Anne got the message. She sat at the table.

'What's he like then—this Australian investigator, Oscar Tremont?' Anne asked.

185

'He's clever, and he's quite a character,' Rowan said. 'If he really has got it all worked out, despite Dad's refusal to be open with him—well, it's amazing.'

Anne muttered something about a stubborn old so-and-so.

'I can't imagine who it could be,' Youna said.

Neither Rowan nor Anne replied.

'He was the kind of man who managed to get on some people's nerves, but to go to all this trouble to dress up and haunt him. That requires pure, scathing hatred, doesn't it?'

'Or wanting to give that impression,' Rowan mused.

His mother frowned, thinking about that, then shrugged it off. 'No idea. When did you last hear from Oscar?'

'This morning, when he called. It was while Major Faure was here. He requested a forensics team.'

Anne's eyebrows arched. 'Where was he?'

Rowan told her and watched his mother's eyebrows drop into a frown.

'Oh, really,' she said slowly, deep in thought. 'Now, that's interesting, isn't it?'

'What does that mean?' Rowan asked impatiently.

'That's the question,' she said quietly, her voice all but drowned out by the growing whistle of the kettle and with a faraway look in her eyes.

'Mum?' Rowan asked loudly.

She snapped out of it and turned to him. 'How many people will be here tonight?'

'He asked for everyone in the village, and Jessica Chotard as well.'

'She's involved?' Anne asked, visibly confused.

'I can't imagine how,' Youna said. 'Your father had nothing to do with her, did he?'

'With a teenage girl?' Rowan asked. 'I should hope not.'

'No,' Anne said. 'The only girls on horseback that interested him were the ones in folk tales and history books. Whatever failings he had, *that* wasn't one of them.'

'We're going to have to wait for this evening,' Youna said.

Rowan prepared a pot of coffee.

'Have you set up the library?' Anne asked. 'This may no longer be my home in any real sense of the word, but if the whole village is coming here this evening, I want them to be welcomed correctly, regardless of the context.'

'I haven't set foot in there since—' Rowan didn't finish the sentence.

'You're going to have to, Rowan,' Anne said, her voice somehow both soft and stern. 'We can't lay him to rest until justice is served, can we?'

Neither Rowan nor Youna replied. They knew Anne was right.

'We'll need at least twenty chairs,' Rowan said eventually, pouring a cup of coffee for his mother. 'I'll look after that.'

'Place them in a semicircle facing your father's desk,' Anne instructed. She sipped carefully at the hot coffee.

'We'll want a chair or two by the door for the gendarmes,' Youna suggested.

'In case the murderer tries to leg it,' Rowan said. 'Good idea.'

'I'll prepare some drinks and *canapés*,' Anne said.

'It's not a dinner party, Mum.'

'All the same, if the whole village is being invited into Ker Greno, I intend to welcome them appropriately,' Anne insisted.

'Even the murderer?'

'Yes, Rowan, even if that means your father's killer gets one last drink before being taken into custody.' She shrugged. 'Is that the end of the world?'

'I guess not,' Rowan admitted. 'I sometimes wish I were more like you.'

Anne gave him a comforting smile.

'You are, Rowan,' Youna assured him. 'I don't know your mum all that well yet, but I can tell you take after her.'

'Thanks,' he said. 'I suppose I've taken the best traits from both of them.'

'Don't push it!' Youna said, and she shared a laugh with Anne.

'I think the last few days have been a learning curve for all of us,'

187

Youna said, but there was an edge of uncertainty to her voice.

'Oh, there's no doubt about it,' Anne assured her. She took a sip of coffee. 'The learning isn't over yet either,' she continued. 'If you're not mistaken about this detective's abilities, Rowan, we're about to find out more about your father than we'd care to know.'

'Whatever it is, we need to know. He's not taking his secrets to the grave.'

'What can I do?' Youna asked.

'About his secrets?' Rowan asked.

'She means about this evening,' Anne said, looking at Youna and rolling her eyes. 'We're women, Rowan. Despite the stereotype, we're the practical sex.'

'Okay, okay,' he said.

'If I prepare a shopping list, would you mind going to the supermarket, Youna?'

'Not at all.'

'Right, let's get to it then,' Anne chirped.

Rowan started gathering chairs in the library, and as he did so, he wondered whether his mother was even the slightest bit sad that her ex-husband was now dead.

#

Once he'd led the forensics team to the grotto, Oscar drove home for lunch, a bath, and a change of clothes. Louise was at work and the boys were at school. He was looking forward to bringing this case to a close and spending time at home again. It had certainly presented a number of challenges, and with two murders taking place under his nose, he couldn't claim it as a clear victory. All the same, he'd been tasked with the job of unmasking the Ankou, and that's what he was about to do—expose the reaper in the presence of the inhabitants of Greno.

David's death got Oscar thinking about his own sons. What lengths would he go to in order to hide his secrets from them? He hoped he'd never find himself in such a position. Were there other

Ankous out there, waiting for the right time?

He took a packet of gyoza from the freezer and a bottle of soy sauce from the fridge. French cuisine was delectable, but there were some habits from Australia he'd kept, like enjoying Asian food every now and then. A light lunch of six fried gyoza accompanied by slices of ginger and a dash of soy sauce was often all he needed to keep him going—accompanied by a glass of red wine, *naturellement*.

Realising he hadn't followed the news recently, he switched the TV on. French political debates and reports on the latest heinous crimes quickly got him down. The irony of that wasn't lost on him, of course, but as strange as it was to admit, however gruesome the murders in Greno were, they belonged to another world. As abominable as it was, it wasn't the mindless violence of domestic abuse and drug trafficking. The main reason he aimed to watch the news every now and then, especially the local broadcasts, was because you simply never knew when the current affairs in some way came into play in a case.

Oscar drank a drop of Bourgueil and ate a slice of pickled ginger while he watched the local news. The bizarre murder of David Trevelyan was the headline. There were shots of Ker Greno taken from the old well and of the dolmen and the woodland path. After the scant details provided by the gendarmerie were given, there was a short explanation about the legend of the Ankou. No interviews with locals. Perhaps no one in the village had wanted to feed the media machine.

While he ate his gyoza and finished the wine, Oscar thought through the next steps to be taken.

#

The black Peugeot 403 came to a halt by the garage at Ker Greno shortly before four o'clock. Oscar had seen little movement on his way into Greno. *Le Chêne* was closed. The was no sign of Major Faure or any of his gendarmes. No journalists either. Nina's car was parked in front of her house, but apart from that, there was nothing

189

to indicate that anyone else was about.

He got out of his car and looked at the white car parked by the salt cedar for a moment. He was looking forward to meeting Rowan's mother at last.

He saw her through the kitchen window as he passed her car. She opened the door to welcome him.

'Oscar Tremont,' she said in impeccable English. 'I've heard so much about you.'

'And I about you.' He winked. 'But not as much, I'm sure, as I'd like to know.'

She feigned shock. 'You think I have secrets, do you?'

'Don't we all?' Oscar asked, and his grin made his moustache twitch mischievously.

'Some more than others,' she said. 'Come in. As per your instructions, we've set the library up for this evening.'

'Thank you so much. I do apologise for not being here when you arrived but I had some loose ends to tie up.'

She looked suitably intrigued.

'Rowan is upstairs?'

'He's with his girlfriend,' Anne said. 'You've spoken to Youna, I suppose.'

Oscar nodded. 'How is he holding up?'

'I don't think he's had enough time to let it sink in. You understand, I'm sure. It hasn't really hit him yet.'

'And you?'

'Me?' Anne asked, raising her eyebrows. 'I'll miss him, and that's the truth.' She remained silent a moment. 'I was madly in love with him once upon a time. This house is full of memories, many of them fond.'

'It must be,' Oscar said softly.

'You met the man, Mister Tremont. You knew him.'

'Ever so briefly.'

'Yes, but you saw what he was like—how stubborn he could be. That's what got him killed. I'll mourn him, and I'll miss him, but there are things I'll never be able to forgive, and this time—this last

190

time—he really outdid himself.' She drew a deep breath. 'Rowan told me what happened. He told me David ignored your instructions. It was kill or be killed.'

'He had no intention of backing down.'

'It's Barbara I feel sorry for.' She leaned a little closer to Oscar. 'I didn't care all that much for Fred myself, between you and me, but she loved her husband, and that—' her voice trailed off. Her point was clear. She frowned at Oscar. 'I don't understand why Fred was killed.'

'All will be known,' he replied.

'It's David's fault Fred is dead.' It wasn't a question.

Oscar merely smiled sympathetically.

'David had secrets and you're going to reveal one of them in a few hours' time. I can't honestly tell you I want to know.'

'I can appreciate that, but know you must. David Trevelyan's life was a puzzle, and it won't be complete until the final piece is in place.'

19. The Ankou is Unmasked

Rowan and Youna began ushering the villagers into the library at a quarter to seven, and Anne showed them where to sit along the two curved rows of chairs Rowan had set up. She offered them refreshments and strove to make everyone feel as comfortable as the circumstances would allow. Gendarmes were posted outside, keeping journalists off the grounds of Ker Greno.

Thérèse was the first to enter the library, and she was very pleased to catch up with Anne, despite the circumstances. She graciously accepted a glass of sparkling wine—just the one, mind you—and complimented Anne on her mini quiches. Nina, who'd left the kids with her parents, joined her shortly later, and one after the other, Kevin, Hervé, Arnaud, and Denise arrived—none with a spring in the step, but one in particular with a bit of a limp. The Chotard family was next, and Anne showed them where to sit at the window end of the first row. Brieg's arrival turned heads, but the big surprise was the return of Barbara. She was dressed soberly in black, but if she'd gathered the strength to be present for the occasion, it wasn't to mourn her husband—which she could do far from the public eye—but to see his killer taken into custody.

Bruno arrived at a minute past seven, thus completing the gathering. Anne showed him where to sit, at the other end of the row from Pascal. There was no point risking further bloodshed in the village.

Once everyone was seated and Major Faure was posted by the door with one of his men, Oscar entered the library and walked slowly to David Trevelyan's desk. He stood with his back to the desk and held his hands in front of him, palms upturned.

'Thank you all for accepting my invitation.'

192

'We didn't have much of a choice, did we?' Brieg boomed, and he grinned as he stroked his goatee. 'If one of us had refused to come, it would be as good as a signed confession.'

Oscar tapped his nose. 'Quite so, Brieg—quite so!'

'The Ankou is here?' Nina asked, unable to hide her apprehension. 'It's really one of us?'

'Let there be no doubt about it—the murderer is here in this very room,' Oscar replied theatrically.

Barbara shifted uneasily in her chair and everyone glanced around suspiciously.

'Who is it?' Hervé asked.

'Bear with me if you will,' Oscar said.

'It's the same person?' Arnaud asked.

Oscar nodded. 'Fred Gaillo and David Trevelyan were indeed murdered by the same person.' He let his gaze fall upon each person seated before him, one after the other. 'However, this evening, it is not two deaths that will be explained, but *three*.'

Gasps and whispers filled the library. Confusion was written on all but two faces—one belonging to the murderer, and the other belonging to Thérèse Derrien. Her expression was one of deep sadness. Her suspicions had now been confirmed.

'Three?' several voices chorused.

'What do you mean?' Denise asked.

Oscar closed his eyes for an instant. When he opened them again, he straightened his moustache between the thumb and forefinger of his right hand.

'Let us begin,' he announced.

Silence reigned, and all eyes were fixed on Oscar Tremont.

'The Ankou came to Greno to claim David Trevelyan's life. Fred Gaillo was not the target. He died because he got in the way.'

Barbara wiped a tear from her eye with a white handkerchief but didn't make a sound. She had resolved not to break down. Her husband's killer didn't deserve the pleasure.

'Fred and our murderer were playing a dangerous game. One of the oldest games in the world—blackmail.'

'Oh, Fred!' Barbara hissed.

'You see, David Trevelyan had quite a few secrets, and one of them was discovered by Fred. Together with the murderer, he hatched a blackmail plan.'

'But?' It was Bruno's voice.

'There was one big problem—' Oscar continued.

They were all ears.

'You can extort or you can seek revenge, but you can't do both.'

'Dead men don't pay!' Brieg called out.

'That's right, my marshland man,' Oscar said. 'As keen as an owl on the prowl. The dead only pay when you're in line to inherit.'

All eyes turned to Rowan.

'This, however, has nothing to do with inheritance. For whatever differences the Trevelyans had, there was no murderous intent in the family. No—the Ankou rode in Greno seeking revenge, not cash.'

'The third death...' Denise said slowly, her mind racing.

'Yes,' Oscar said. 'The third death. That was the key piece to this puzzle, and it brings us to the point where our murderer must be unmasked.'

There were no whispers or murmurs now. Thérèse Derrien knew what was coming, and Oscar saw that the murderer was the focus of Jessica Chotard's gaze.

'This is your last chance to stand up and confess of your own free will,' Oscar said, looking at no one in particular.

Several people shifted uncomfortably, but the killer didn't move an inch.

'No?' Oscar asked. 'I'll not do as certain other detectives are wont to do. I'll not cast false accusations for dramatic effect before revealing the identity of the Ankou. That wouldn't be fair on any of you, and especially not on those of you who are suffering right now.' He looked at Rowan, and then offered Barbara a sympathetic smile.

'We're ready to hear it, Oscar,' Rowan said. 'Barbara?'

She nodded. 'Who is it? Unmask the monster!'

Oscar swept the gathering with his gaze, but it eventually fell upon the blank, unsuspecting face of Denise Guivarc'h.

He released a sigh. 'I'm so sorry for you,' he told her.

Her heart broke at that moment, and she turned to her son, shaking her head.

'It's all lies, Mum!' Hervé spat, staring at Oscar, because he couldn't bear to look his mother in the eye.

Gasps filled the library.

'Hervé?' Kevin asked. 'Tell me it's not true!'

'All lies!' Hervé insisted.

Oscar shook his head.

'You don't have any proof!' Hervé yelled, getting to his feet and pointing at Oscar, but Major Faure and his gendarme were beside him now.

He sat, crossed his arms, and kept his mouth shut.

'Oh, there's plenty of proof,' Oscar announced, addressing the assembly. 'More than enough.'

Everyone was listening intently, Hervé most of all. Denise held her son by the hand. There was little else she could do.

'The secret Fred discovered was that of a hidden treasure found in a grotto not far from Ranrouët Castle.'

Denise let go of her son's hand and clasped her hands over her mouth. She stared at Oscar wide-eyed.

'Christophe didn't run away with another woman?' Anne asked.

'He did not,' Oscar confirmed. 'David Trevelyan and Christophe Guivarc'h found the fabled Revolution treasure buried near Ranrouët Castle. We may never know exactly what happened, but forensics are examining the remains that were buried there.'

'Oh, my—' Anne began. 'I knew he had his secrets, but I never took David for a murderer.'

'We don't know how it happened,' Oscar repeated. 'Perhaps we never will. David had a scar on the back of his head, and he turned white when I mentioned it. Why? I believe he got it at Ranrouët. Was there a fight? Did Christophe try to kill him or knock him out so he could make off with the treasure, but David fought back? We

195

can only speculate. What we do know for sure—what Fred and Hervé discovered—was that David left that hollow alive, and Christophe didn't.'

'That sounds like murder to me,' Pascal declared, not looking at Bruno but knowing everyone present would understand the comparison he was making with the hunting accident that had claimed his son's life.

'I'm so sorry, Denise,' Anne said, and then she turned to Rowan, who was speechless.

Hervé still sat with his arms crossed, doing his best not to react.

'Fred found a map in the dovecote in the garden. He left it in place so David wouldn't suspect anything, but I found it, much to Hervé's dismay. That kick to the face really hurt!'

'Baseless accusations,' Hervé said, before going back to being silent.

'You almost left a boot print on my forehead.'

Hervé shrugged, unimpressed.

'Not to worry—those you left in your neighbour's vegetable garden will match those boots you're wearing.'

'What has Thérèse's vegetable garden got to do with any of this?' Arnaud asked, trying not to laugh.

'We'll get to that in a moment,' Oscar said without a hint of amusement in his voice. 'Firstly, we need to understand what happened to Fred Gaillo. He wanted money. Hervé, on the other hand, found himself in Hamlet's shoes and yearned to avenge his father's death. These goals were incompatible. There was only one possible outcome. Fred had to die—and so he did.

'Killing Fred and disposing of his body wasn't enough though, was it? This was an opportunity too good to be missed. A severed head placed on the dolmen would push David Trevelyan to the brink of madness. Before he died, he needed to be punished—tormented. That's the whole reason Hervé went to so much trouble to become the Ankou. David's life had been dedicated to Breton folklore, and so what better death for him than a folkloric one? He was sentenced to be harrowed before being harvested.'

The library was as silent as the grave for what felt like an eternity.

Kevin broke the spell. 'You're saying Fred was killed elsewhere and his severed head placed on the dolmen during the night?'

'That is correct. I can't give all my secrets away, but I know no one came along the woodland path that night. Fred was killed in the marshland but his head was placed on the dolmen by someone approaching from the village. That in itself indicated the likelihood of someone living in a house with access to the marshes at the back of the garden.'

Oscar looked around to make sure everyone was following, but there were some confused faces.

'How do you know he was killed in the marshes?' Rowan asked.

'My thanks to Brieg for confirming my suspicions on this point. His intimate knowledge of the marshes came in very handy. You see, there was a grey feather on the ground near the dolmen. It was the one and only clue carelessly left behind. It was the feather of a grey bird only found in the marshes. It shouldn't have been near the village.'

'A heron?' Pascal asked.

'Precisely. I deduced that the feather had been at the scene of the murder and was somehow transported with Fred's head to the dolmen.'

'In a sack of some kind,' Kevin suggested.

'That's what I guessed, and the logical assumption was that the sack would be found in a safe place, in the cart stolen from Pascal's farm.'

'His cart hasn't been found,' Nina reminded him.

Oscar saw the smug grin on Hervé's face—it wouldn't last long.

'Oh, I found it,' Oscar said casually.

Hervé's face went pale.

'How?'

'It seemed obvious it would be nearby,' Oscar said. 'Somewhere in the marshes—accessible but hidden. But how can you hide a cart in plain sight on solid ground?'

No one answered.

'No ideas?'

'Behind bushes,' Brieg said, stroking his goatee.

Oscar clicked his fingers. 'Yes. The problem is getting the cart through the screen of bushes without crushing and snapping them.' He narrowed his eyes at Hervé. 'Then I remembered Fred was a talented gardener and that he'd done a spot of landscaping. A man like that probably had a trick or two up his sleeves. Tricks that anyone who had worked with him might know.'

Hervé was looking less cocky by the minute, but he hadn't yet heard any solid proof against him.

'A row of bushes was planted between the track linking Greno and Kergaillot and a stretch of disused track passing along the edge of the marshland. There were three small holly bushes appearing to block what would otherwise have been the entrance to that disused track. The bushes were not, however, planted directly in the ground but in large cloth sacks placed in holes. With leaves and grass around the base, it looked like they were growing naturally, but these three plants could easily be removed and put back into place again later. Damned clever, I have to admit.'

'He couldn't have left a horse there with it,' Pascal said. 'Someone would have noticed—I for one.'

'This is where it gets interesting,' Oscar said, noticing that Thérèse was already looking at Jessica, but he knew her thoughts were with Denise. 'Can you come up, Jessica? If that's all right with your parents.'

'Of course,' she said, without even waiting for either of them to reply. She took her place by Oscar's side, standing straight with her shoulders back.

'You all know Jessica, right?' Oscar asked.

'We do.' It was Youna. 'Are you saying Minuit was the Ankou's steed?'

'Beyond a shadow of a doubt.'

'How is Hervé supposed to have got Minuit to come along with him and drawn the cart?' Kevin asked, not at all convinced.

Oscar turned to Jessica. She smiled and nodded.

'More easily than you might think,' Jessica began. 'She's familiar with carts and she's friendly. All you need is a little confidence and a good supply of carrots.'

'A good supply of carrots?' Oscar asked, turning to Thérèse. 'We know Madame Derrien has been complaining about someone stealing her carrots. We now know it was her next-door neighbour, Hervé. The plaster cast I took of one of the boot prints leading from the base of the dividing wall to where her carrots grow will match.'

'You can tell that from there, can you?' Hervé asked.

'I can,' Oscar replied flatly.

'There's a problem with this—hypothesis,' Arnaud pointed out.

'Minuit's white streak?' Oscar asked.

'Exactly. I heard the horse was completely black.'

'This is where Jessica's insight proved invaluable. While Brieg knows everything there is to know about waterfowl, marshland fauna, and wild mushrooms, Jessica is quite the young expert on husbandry and grooming.' He turned to her.

'There are several products readily available from country stores—or online—which enable you to easily cover white spots on a horse's coat. These creams can be applied and removed without much bother.'

Oscar walked around the desk and bent to pick up something hidden behind it. He walked back to Jessica, holding the plastic bag containing a small white tub up for everyone to see. There was a black horse on the label, and the words; *Make-up Black*.

'Did you find and provide me with tiny traces of a product like this found around the edges of Minuit's white streak?'

'I did,' Jessica confirmed.

'No matter how much you scratch and scrub, there's always a minute amount left behind. The same goes for both horses and humans.' Oscar indicated Hervé's hands.

Hervé looked at his fingernails and frowned.

'I have no doubt that matching traces will be detected under his fingernails. The police are very good at that kind of thing when they

199

happen to look in the right place.'

Major Faure cleared his throat loudly.

'By the way, how's your left leg, Hervé?' Oscar asked casually. 'You should get that wound seen to.'

Without losing a beat, he strode around the desk and fetched a dirty sack. 'As Kevin rightly pointed out, Fred's head—and I'm so sorry to have to speak so tactlessly, Barbara, but we need the details—was most likely carried in a sack. This is the sack I retrieved from the cart.'

Hervé was looking hopeless now.

'The Ankou's trappings were inside.'

The library was again filled with gasps and murmurs as Oscar removed each bagged item one by one—the black hat, the coachman's gloves, the skull mask, and the tea tin.

'There will be DNA on those items,' Major Faure announced.

'Yes,' Oscar said. 'But that's not all.' He paused for dramatic effect. 'When I was at the grotto near Ranrouët Castle and I opened the toolbox I found there, I saw a skull that forensics will confirm belonged to Christophe Guivarc'h. Call it twisted romanticism if you like, but I realised with a chill that the contours of the skull and the contours of the mask are eerily similar—in fact, they are identical.'

The assembly was speechless for a second.

Oscar nodded slowly and looked at Hervé.

'You're saying he cast the mask from his father's skull?' Pascal asked, a hint of admiration in his voice.

'Yes. He wore the mask in his father's name. It was their *revenge mask.*'

'Oh, Hervé,' Denise sobbed.

No one spoke.

'There is one final detail that didn't escape my attention,' Oscar said. 'At the shrine to Christophe Guivarc'h, there is a rusty garden gate. Photographs of the village show this gate was once the entrance to Denise and Hervé's front garden.'

'Hervé replaced it with the new pine one,' Denise mused. 'He told me he'd taken the old one to the scrapyard. Why, Hervé—why?'

Major Faure was looking intently at Oscar now. There was a look of admiration mingled with annoyance on his face. It was a look Oscar was familiar with.

Oscar nodded and the major strode over and did his duty.

Hervé Guivarc'h was taken into custody.

20. Home for Halloween

Oscar looked the witch up and down. Pointed black hat, the tip flopping to one side. Plastic nose even more prominent than the real one. Hairy wart on the chin—fake, of course. Black web cape wrapped around a long black dress of coarse material. Purple leggings with black bat pattern. Worn black boots with pointed toes and silver buckles—from her everyday wardrobe, not the costume shop. Straw broom, usually used for sweeping up household dirt, not as a means of transport. Glass of prosecco—

He frowned. 'I didn't know Italian sparkling was part of a witch's kit.'

Louise winked. 'This witch likes it. What would you have me drinking—elderberry wine?'

Oscar's moustache twitched. 'Now that's a thought. There's elderberry growing in the garden. I'll have to make some for next year.'

'I don't know that I'll be dressing up as a witch next year,' Louise pointed out.

'No, but we both know you'll have a glass of something or other at your lips.'

They laughed.

'Apart from the prosecco, am I convincing as a witch?'

Oscar opened his mouth to speak, but thought better of it and sipped his stout instead.

'Careful,' Louise warned.

'Relatively convincing,' he said diplomatically.

She did her best witch giggle, and it actually sent a shiver down Oscar's spine.

'Let's have a look at you then,' she said, giving him the once-over.

He donned his dun-coloured mask with pointy ears and two huge and yellowed canines sticking up from behind a thick lower lip, then he held his arms out and turned around slowly, making sure not to spill a drop of the Irish stout.

He was wearing a green-brown tunic with a thick leather belt around the waist and a pair of brown corduroys. His shoes were hidden under dirty rags.

'What *exactly* are you supposed to be?'

'Isn't it obvious?'

'I really can't tell. Is it a Breton monster?'

'Not on your life!' Oscar said a little more loudly than he'd intended. 'I need a break from all that for a while. Think further north.'

'Belgian—like your beer?'

Oscar tutted. 'Really, Louise, haven't I taught you anything? This is an O'Hara's Dry.'

'Oh, Ireland then?'

'The stout, yes, but not the costume. Think Scandinavia.'

She looked at him blankly and he got the feeling she'd whack him with her broom if he didn't stop trying to make her guess.

'I'm a troll.'

'Oh.'

'*Oh*—is that all? I went to all this effort and that's your reaction? Forget it, where are the boys?'

'Getting into character. They'll be down soon.'

'I'm glad I got the case wrapped up in time for Halloween.'

'So are the boys.' She smiled. 'So am *I*, Oscar. What a bizarre affair!'

'It was. It's all over now though. What's done is done.'

'You've put a dangerous man behind bars. I'm proud of you.'

'I know,' he said, a little too thoughtfully for a troll.

'Boys!' Louise shouted.

'We're almost ready,' they chorused.

Louise turned back to her husband and touched the tip of his monstrous rubber nose with the long purple nail of her index finger.

'I was worried you wouldn't want to celebrate Halloween at all after such a haunting case.'

He slipped his mask up just enough to allow himself to take a sip of stout. 'Miss out on enjoying the one evening of the year those two monsters can really be themselves and let their lights—or lanterns, as it were—shine. There was no way in the world I was going to do that, Louise.'

'I can't stop thinking about that poor boy,' she admitted. 'He's going to have to be very *courageux*.'

'He's a strong-minded young man,' Oscar told her. 'What's more, he has two wonderful women in his life—perhaps three, but I didn't get the chance to meet his sister.'

'That's reassuring.'

'We've agreed to stay in touch. I plan on checking in on him from time to time.'

Louise smiled, far too sweetly for such a wicked witch.

Footsteps sounded on the floorboards just then and the younger of the boys came rushing downstairs to join his parents. He was dressed as a skeleton wrapped in chains. The costume was convincing. The skeleton looked like it had only moments earlier emerged from the dungeon of a ruined castle for the first time in centuries. There was a treasure chest in one hand and a blood-spattered axe in the other.

Once the skeleton had reached the foot of the stairs, the next set of footsteps sounded—slower, heavier, more ominous.

'Beware! The Reaper rides tonight!' the skeleton announced.

The long black robe came into view first, and Oscar watched transfixed as Death descended. When he caught sight of the skull half-hidden under the black hood, he felt a quick shiver run through his body.

'The harvest moon shines red on this darkest of evenings. Let the reaping begin!' Death declared solemnly, and it swung its scythe, narrowly missing the troll's pint glass.

'You told them, Louise?'

The witch looked the troll in the eye and tutted before deigning to reply. 'I did not. I didn't have to tell them. It's been all over the news, Oscar.'

'Cool scythe, isn't it?' Death asked, its voice chirpy this time.

'Very cool,' Oscar heard himself saying. 'It almost looks real.'

'I reckon I could lop a head off with this thing.'

'Let's not try that,' Oscar answered, staring at the curved blade. 'Best we keep our reaping to treats.'

For news, reviews, competitions, author interviews, and exclusive excerpts

Visit our website
blackbeaconbooks.com

Like us on Facebook
facebook.com/BlackBeaconBooks

Join us on Twitter
@BlackBeacons

Find us on Instagram
instagram.com/blackbeaconbooks

Subscribe on Patreon
patreon.com/blackbeaconbooks

Discover all our Social Media Links
https://linktr.ee/blackbeaconbooks

www.ingramcontent.com/pod-product-compliance
Lightning Source LLC
Chambersburg PA
CBHW021144130626
46554CB00005B/1656